Forbidden Fruit

Forbidden Fruit

Liz Merritt

Copyright © 2009 by Liz Merritt.

Library of Congress Control Number: 2009902073
ISBN: Hardcover   978-1-4415-1696-1
               Softcover   978-1-4415-1695-4

All rights reserved. No part of this book may be reproduced or transmitted in any form or by any means, electronic or mechanical, including photocopying, recording, or by any information storage and retrieval system, without permission in writing from the copyright owner.

This is a work of fiction. Names, characters, places and incidents either are the product of the author's imagination or are used fictitiously, and any resemblance to any actual persons, living or dead, events, or locales is entirely coincidental.

This book was printed in the United States of America.

To order additional copies of this book, contact:
Xlibris Corporation
1-888-795-4274
www.Xlibris.com
Orders@Xlibris.com
54580

CHAPTER 1

Spring was about to arrive, and Rebecca could not wait. She had prepared most of the winter for her things that she would sell at the market. It had been a really tough winter for her, and she was so looking forward to venturing out into the other world again. It had been almost a year now since she had lost her husband, Daniel. It was hard to believe that the time had passed so quickly; however, she felt almost guilty for not missing him anymore. It had not been an arranged marriage, but among the Amish, your choices were mostly the ones your father gave you. She had been nineteen and committed to the Ordnung when her father, Samuel Fisher, had decided that she would marry Daniel Lapp. She was not against the marriage, for he seemed like a good man and would make a good husband. She was excited about her new life as a wife and mother. It was not until a few months into the marriage that she knew that she and Daniel were not right for each other. She had no feelings for him other than like those that she felt for her brothers. She was ashamed and horrified to the reality that unless something drastically changed, she would live her whole life in a loveless marriage. Daniel, although he had never said anything, felt the same. They had spent their wedding night almost in silence. It was near dawn when Daniel mustered enough courage to try his first attempts at lovemaking. It had not been what she thought it was going to be. Afterward, she got up and started breakfast, and he started his chores. There were no declarations of love or any kind of a flame. She did not know too much about the art, but she was told by her mother, Mary, on their wedding day that all she needed to know was that is what was necessary to have children. She was grateful that she had not gotten pregnant during the first few months. She was almost sure it was the infrequent lovemaking sessions though.

Daniel had been finishing their barn with their fathers and brothers when he fell. He broke his neck in the fall. She mourned for the loss of a friend and for the sake of others but silently thanked God for saving her from the mistake that she had made. She asked for forgiveness for this but never spoke of this matter to anyone. She was a very quiet person anyway. After her rumspringa, she took the oath of the Amish. She had done so because that was all that she had ever known. She had never told anyone of the secret that she daydreamed often. She always had a desire to live in the English world. All the years of traveling with her father and mother, she would long to dress as the worldly women did. She had also seen men that she thought to be extremely handsome. In the Amish community, it is forbidden to admire the way someone looked or to put anything into a person's physical features. A man was known as whether he was a good husband and father material, and a woman was sought after because she would make a good wife and mother. She had never thought of herself as pretty at all. Her hair was blonde and, despite her efforts, hung straight as a board when she took it down to wash and comb it. Her eyes were very blue, just like her father's. She had a clear complexion, but for some reason, she thought herself to be very unattractive. She had a petite build, and her bosom was so big her mother bound them with a material to make them look smaller. "Women were supposed to dress modest," she said. Daniel had never seen her without clothes the whole time they were married, but she knew this was not common among the Amish. Their lovemaking was done behind locked doors in the dark of night.

She had spent the winter in the company of her two younger brothers John and Amos. Her father had sent them to help with the chores that she could not do. They were not yet of marrying age, and although she was sure Father had missed their help, she knew that her older brother David was more than capable help for her father. He was going to announce his marriage intentions this year. She had wanted her younger sister Sarah to come and stay as well, but her father thought that was not a good idea. Sarah was good help to her mother and was not finished with school. She stood at the kitchen window as she watched her brothers feed the livestock. They wrestled and played joyfully as they went about their chores. She wanted to be joyful again, but she was trying to honor Daniel and, thus, mourn him for a full year. When John and Amos came bursting in the kitchen, it startled her out of the daydream she was in. "Becca, are you all right?" John asked. "I am sorry we scared you." "No, no, I am fine, my brothers, you just startled me, that's all. Now sit yourselves down and eat your breakfast before it gets cold." John and Amos began their meal with the normal prayer, which John, as the elder male, extended. When they had finished the prayer and began eating, John said, "I am going to make the repairs on your buggy, sis. She will bring you to market just fine." "Father says I am going with you this year," Amos said excitedly. "He says you don't need to be by yourself." Rebecca smiled and said, "Well, we wouldn't dare argue with Father now, would we?" She winked at him and tossed her blonde hair in his face. She loved her family very much. There were nine of them altogether. David was the firstborn, and then her, John, Amos, Steven, Sarah, Paul, Katie, and finally little Annie. Annie was only five, and Rebecca loved her so. She often came and stayed with her as well. Rebecca's farm was not but a few miles from her mother and father, thus, making visiting easy. The winter had been a particular harsh one, so she visited as often as the weather allowed. When John and Amos had finished eating, they started toward the door. Rebecca playfully threw the kitchen towel in their direction and said, "What, no help with the dishes, you two?" John smiled at her and put his black hat on his head. She watched out the window as they gathered their seed sacks and headed to the field to plot the garden that would provide her with the money to support herself. She knew she would probably be expected to take a husband this winter, but she tried not to think about that too much. She knew because she was not a virgin anymore, she would be chosen by one of the old widowers of the community. Her father had already made mention of Ezekiel King. He had lost his wife to pneumonia three years ago. He had taken her to the hospital one afternoon after he knew it was more than a bad cold. However, after a week's hospital stay, she still went to be with the Lord. He had been left with a daughter, Mary Grace. He was not a bad-looking man. But the thought of getting married again was more than she could bear for now.

The next few weeks were spent finishing her needlework she was going to sell at the market. She had quite a bit of canned fruits and vegetables she had prepared, and everything was coming together nicely. She had worked very hard, and she hoped it would pay off. She had spent most of the day cleaning and packing her produce and was extremely tired. She ate a quick supper and climbed into bed. She drifted off to sleep in no time. She woke up suddenly with her body warm and moist with sweat. When her breathing had returned to normal, she lay in her bed wondering what had just happened. She had dreamed of being with a man intimately, and as he made love to her sweetly, he whispered her name in her ear. She had a feeling come over her that she had never had before. It was a wonderful feeling. She felt most sure that this was the way a woman who was fully satisfied in bed felt. She had gotten bits and pieces of information by her friends and occasionally hearing some of the women talk about their experiences. This was not a subject that anyone was supposed to talk of however. This was only necessary to have children and never was supposed to be looked at as something pleasurable. Therefore, it did not matter if women were satisfied or not. She lay there and wiped the sweat that was on her forehead with the back of her hand. She threw the covers that were near her away to the bottom of the bed. It was a full moon, and the light shone through her bedroom window. She could not help but notice the peaks that were so perfectly erect and pushing against her nightgown, begging to be released. She untied the string that held her gown together. As it fell, her naked breasts were exposed. The cool breeze of the cracked window felt wonderful to her. It kissed her moist skin, and although the material was thin, she thought how good it would feel if it was off. Wondering if she should dare, she sat up and pulled the gown from over her head. She lay their on her bed with her body drinking the breeze of the cool early spring night. Her body was still heated from the dream. She replayed how this stranger held her so sweetly yet so firmly as he whispered her name in her ear. Her body tingled with delight each time she replayed it in her mind, making it extremely hard to find sleep again. She wanted to desperately; she wanted to see if she could go back to the same dream. She lay there for what seemed to be hours, thinking about her dream and then eventually remembered that it was her first day to sell at the market. She had gotten up and dressed quickly. When she had almost finished cooking breakfast, Amos came sleepily to the table. The sun was not yet up, but this is the time that the day started when you live as they live. There is truly not enough hours in a day to get everything done. They had eaten their breakfast quickly and began to load the wagon. When everything had been checked thoroughly and Rebecca was satisfied that her buggy was secure, she hopped up and grabbed the reins. She saw the strange look on Amos's face and said, "Here, brother dear, you want to drive us today?" Amos smiled brightly at her and reined the horse forward. The gelding had been Daniel's, but he was quite good with it in town traffic. The noise from the passing cars never spooked him, and he was a beautiful animal. Rebecca smiled sweetly as she thought about the day ahead. She loved the market and meeting the people. She especially loved getting to be out in the outside world. After their twenty-mile journey, they had finally reached the market. Amos pulled the buggy up to the tent where her father had instructed her to go, and Amos began to unload the produce as she hung her needlework for display. When everything was ready to be sold, Rebecca lifted the curtain on the tent. It was about seven when the first of the customers began to congregate. By eight, the crowd had doubled, and everyone was busy as could be. Rebecca was getting a pair of pillowcases that she had embroidered, down from a hanging display when she caught a glimpse of this man. She nearly fell from her ladder she was standing on but quickly caught herself. She regained her composure and finished the sale. As the day unfolded and Rebecca only had a few items left, as destiny would have it, the man appeared again. She watched as he walked toward her tent. She caught her breath as she got a good look at him. "The man from my dream last night!" she said to herself. He walked in and began to look around. He looked at the produce and made his selection. Rebecca couldn't take her eyes off him. She had to keep reminding herself to look away. She did not want to be caught looking at him so intently. Amos would no doubt go tell everyone, and if her father caught her, she would never be allowed back at the market. The thought of that made her blood boil. When he went over to inspect her needlework, he said, "Excuse me, may I ask a question?" It was all Rebecca could do to answer. "Yes, of course, you may!" she answered nervously. When she looked onto his eyes, she was taken aback by the effect they had on her. She was sure that she had blushed from it. She quickly fanned herself and said, "Did you have a question, sir?" Cade Matthews was a handsome man. He had shoulder-length black hair that fell across his face. His eyes were olive green, which were outlined with black that made them stand out even more. He was twenty-five and spent a lot of time in the gym. He had never married and, for some reason, had never really found anyone that he even cared to date. He had seen Rebecca several times that day, and from the first moment he saw her, he was intrigued. He could not seem to make himself leave although it had taken him most of the day to gather enough nerve to go over to her tent. He knew nothing about sewing, and he had to try to come up with some questions that seem legitimate to ask. He was not going to ask, "Is this produce fresh?" that would make him look like a complete idiot! He finally decided that honesty was best, and mustering enough courage, he headed out. "Do you know what size these pillowcases are? My mother's birthday is this week, and these are really nice. I thought these would make a great gift!" Cade looked down at her as he talked. Her eyes were the clearest blue that he had ever seen.

She was very petite; however, she was, from what he could tell, very well built. Her hair was a beautiful blonde, and he could easily imagine it hanging down across her face and chest. "Yes, these are standard size. They will fit a twin- or full-size bed," she answered, still trying to pull her gaze away. Cade stammered for another question so he could stand there a minute longer. "Well, do you have another design maybe?" Rebecca turned and walked over in another direction. Cade was following her, and as she turned to leave, he could not help himself. He caught a glimpse of her backside. He could imagine what it may look like although the dress that she wore gave little hint of its size. She stopped and grabbed her ladder and continued over to another corner of the tent. As she climbed the ladder to retrieve another set of pillowcases, she got overbalanced and was about to fall. Cade done what any gentleman would do in that situation—he grabbed her to steady her. When he touched her, she burst into flames and panicked all at the same time. She knew that was forbidden, and her father would be there shortly. She grabbed the ladder and said breathlessly, "Oh, forgive me, sir, I am far too clumsy today." "No! I mean, um, I am sorry if I have offended you in any way. Tell your husband that I meant no disrespect. I was trying to keep you from falling." Samuel was there before he had took his hands away. He held out his hand to help his daughter down from the ladder. "Thank you, sir, for helping my daughter. I think I will get her brother to hang these lower so there will be no need for a ladder." Rebecca's face was red as the beets she was selling. She knew that her father would speak to her about this, and she hoped she could keep her feelings from showing. When she had realized what she had said, she was infuriated with herself. *Feelings! What feelings! You idiot, you just met the man!* Samuel, once again turning his attention to the stranger, said, "Thank you again, Mr . . . uh?" "Oh! Matthews, Cade Matthews." "Thank you again, Mr. Matthews, for helping my daughter." He turned and said, "Rebecca, get your brother to hang these lower and put this ladder away before you do get hurt." She smiled and nodded in agreement with her father, and as Amos was walking up, he had already heard the request of his father and had immediately turned to start lowering the items. Rebecca turned and said, "Would you be wanting these, Mr. Matthews?" He was surprised that she had remembered his name. He quickly answered, "Yes, I would like both sets, thank you." As she was bagging the items that he had purchased for him, he asked, "Are you going to be here every Saturday?" She smiled and answered, "Yes, until the fall." He took the bag from her hand, and when their hands touched briefly, he smiled and said, "Good . . . I mean if my mother likes these and wants to buy more, I know where I can get them, right?" Rebecca giggled and replied, "Yes, thank you!" Cade turned and walked away, nodding to her father as he left. When he had returned to his car, he watched as her father walked over and pulled her to the back of the tent. He observed as he was sure that her father was not happy at what had just transpired. He sat pretending to talk on his phone as to not draw any more attention to himself. "Did you hear me, Becca?" Rebecca's eyes were at her feet as her father was speaking to her. She answered, "Yes, Father, I hear you, it was an accident. I guess I have not been sleeping well, and I am a little tired." "Well, get you some rest and be more careful, daughter," he said in a hushed voice. He did not want to draw attention to the situation any further. Rebecca watched as Cade left and secretly hoped that she would see him again. The day passed by quickly, and she prepared her unsold items for the trip home. Amos and John had to help their father with some heavy chores the next day, so they had ridden in the wagon with him. When they reached her driveway, she waved good night and reined her buggy toward the barn. As she readied the buggy for the night and unhitched the horse, she could not get Cade Matthews off her mind. The way his hands felt around her tiny waist. Just the thought of it made her tingle all over. She finished her chores in the barn and continued to the house. Once inside all alone, she could daydream all she wanted. After she had eaten her supper, she lay on the couch to rest a moment and drifted off to sleep. She once again met her beautiful stranger in dreamland. This time, the lovemaking had been much more passionate and had awakened her. She sat upright quickly and tried to slow her labored breathing. The dream had been so real it had left her body wet with perspiration. She decided that a warm bath would feel really nice. She made her way upstairs and settled into a tub of water. She soaked for what seemed to be an hour, and the water had left her shivering from the coolness of it. She dried off and headed to bed. She had a big day tomorrow and wanted to get started preparing her stuff for next week's market. She lay across the bed hoping that she would get to see the man that she could not keep from her thoughts. She fell asleep thinking of Cade.

The next morning, she made herself a pot of coffee and began making plans of what she would carry to the market for the coming week. She ate her breakfast, making notes, and then went to feed the livestock. When she was finished, she went upstairs to clean up from the dirty job. Although it was forbidden to have mirrors, she had purchased a small one from the store one afternoon when she had been dropped off by her father. She had wrapped it carefully and kept it on a shelf in her closet. Rebecca often got it down and tried new hairstyles when no one was around. Her hair was the color of the silk that grew in the corn each year. Although most did not speak of whether it was pretty or not, Daniel had told her one night that her hair was beautiful. She had taken it down to bath and was brushing it when he came to bed. It was very shiny, and when let down, it touched the small of her back. She decided she would try to French braid it this week. Most of the Amish women parted theirs down the middle and balled it into their bonnets. However, just in case Cade did return this week, she wanted to look her best without drawing any attention. She knew her father would be furious and forbid her to return to the market. She had no choice in her clothing; all she had was the uniform of the Amish women. She always wore a black skirt with a royal blue long-sleeve blouse that was tucked in with a long black pinafore apron. The dress was to cover the ankles, and her hair was to be in her bonnet at all times. There were no exceptions even when she was at home. She remembered during her rumspringa that she had adorned the clothes of an Englishwoman one time when she had gone with a friend out one night. Her friend and some others gathered to watch some movies with a crowd of other teens her age. She loved them—the jeans had fit her curves well, and the T-shirt she wore had shown the fullness of her bosom. After the initial shock had worn off, she was very pleased with her body. It was just her face that she had a problem with. She never felt she measured up to the worldly women at all. That had been a major deciding factor that drove her back to the Amish way of life. She knew she would not have to worry about her physical appearance at all. She was admired for her ability to run a home. Rebecca knew hands down that she could do that well. Her mother had been a kind, patient women and was excellent at everything it took to run a home. She had been a good teacher, and she had learned well. Rebecca took her beautiful long hair down from her bonnet and began to brush it. She had propped the mirror up on a shelf in her bathroom so she could see her reflection. She fixed her hair in many different ways before deciding on what she would do with it. After all, there could be no drastic change or her father would suspect her intentions. She had finished putting it back up when she heard someone at the door. She carefully wrapped the mirror and returned it to the shelf before she went to answer the door. Rebecca pulled the curtain back to where she could see who was at her door and suddenly panicked when she saw Ezekiel King, standing and straightening his hat. *Oh no! What should I do!* she thought as her hands went over her mouth.

She was positive that he had talked to her father about courting her. She knew now that he had chosen today to do so. She quickly messed her hair up a little and opened the door. "Hello, Ezekiel, how are you today?" she said in a very tired-sounding voice. "I am good, Rebecca, thank you for asking. May I have a word with you out on the porch?" Ezekiel asked firmly. Rebecca nodded her head in agreement and joined him. "Ezekiel, I am sorry I don't have long, I am very busy today preparing for the market," she said, wiping her hands on her apron. He smiled graciously at her and said, "I don't want to keep you from your chores, I just wanted to offer you something. I know your Daniel had been gone awhile now, and I hate seeing you run this place by yourself. I wish to tell you that if you would agree to it, I want to make you my wife this winter. You don't have to answer me now. Just think on it a while. In the meantime, I will come as often as I can and help with your place, and if there is anything you need, I would be happy to do it for you." Rebecca felt her face flush, for the life of her, she did not know why. She quietly replied, "Ezekiel, I thank you very much, and I will think on it, but please don't be letting your own chores go lacking to come do mine. My brothers are good helpers, and as you can see, I am managing fine. That is very kind of you though for thinking of me." She turned to face the barn so he could not see how embarrassed she was. She felt like a fresh loaf of bread out of the oven. When she had regained her composure, she continued, "I would ask you to stay for a cup of coffee, but I am afraid you caught me off guard and busy." Ezekiel, who had his hat resting on his chest in respect to her, answered, "I am sorry for coming unannounced, but I have been thinking on this awhile, and I wanted to speak to you about it. I will leave you now and let you continue with your chores. If it is okay, I will return toward the end of the week." "Ezekiel, I am honored that you have given me consideration, really I am. I just want you to understand I am not sure I am ready to marry again," she said, trying to spare his feelings. "I understand, Rebecca, and I do appreciate you being honest about it. However, until you make your mind up, I would like to help you," Ezekiel said, pleading. "As long as we have this understanding and you know how I feel, that will be fine," Rebecca answered firmly. "Well, I guess I will leave now and let you get back to your chores," Ezekiel said as he started down the stairs. "I will be seeing you." Rebecca watched from the porch as he climbed into his buggy and was pulling away. He was a very nice man; however, she was certain that she did not want to enter another marriage with no feelings other than friendship. She longed to be held by a man that could bring all those passion-filled feelings alive. She felt dead herself, and she longed to be awakened. She returned to the kitchen where she poured herself another cup of coffee and began making her list of supplies from the store. She grabbed her sweater and went to the barn to hitch the buggy. Rebecca decided today she would travel to town by herself. She knew her father did not like for her to travel without a chaperon. He and her brothers were very busy today planting the potatoes and other crops that had to be laid in early. She was only going to a local grocery store for a few items anyway. She was about to finish purchasing what was on her list when she rounded an aisle and bumped into someone. "Cade! I mean, Mr. Matthews, I am so sorry!" Rebecca said, quickly correcting herself. She was shocked at seeing him, and she was sure that he saw the excitement in her face. "Rebecca, what a wonderful surprise. I am so glad to see you. I ran out of coffee, and for someone that works from home at all hours of the day and night, that is something you do not want to be without," Cade said as he smiled brightly. "I love coffee too! It helps me get started every day," she said in a nervous tone. "I hope that your father was not too angry with me the other day. Nor your husband, I meant no harm," Cade stated. "Oh, it is okay. My father was only trying to keep me from gossip, and I am not married, my husband died almost a year ago now," she said, trying not to sound as though she were dropping a hint. "Oh, I am sorry, Rebecca! I am sure that was hard on you," Cade said, trying not to sound too excited. Rebecca could tell by his tone that he was glad to hear that she was not married. This excited her beyond words. She knew that if she were caught talking to him by someone of her community, she would be in big trouble; however, she could not pull herself away. "Thank you, Mr. Matthews, that is kind of you," she said. "Oh, please call me Cade if that is okay for you to do that. I have been doing some reading on the Amish, and I am amazed. I have only just started, but I find it fascinating," he said as he watched her face. Rebecca blurted it out, "I can't imagine why." She turned red and suddenly got very nervous. Rebecca knew that she had revealed her true feelings to him. Cade could not believe his ears. He had been intrigued by this woman ever since he had laid eyes on her. He could not, for the life of him, stop thinking about her. "So tell me, Rebecca, do you live alone?" Cade asked. "Yes, I do, my brothers come help. I have a big family, so there is always enough help when you need it!" Cade laughed at her attempt to be funny. He watched as she talked, and he wanted so badly to touch her. She was beautiful and had an innocence about her that made her even more beautiful. He watched her full lips as she talked with a German dialect. He could not help noticing her beautiful crystal blue eyes that showed her emotion as she talked. He imagined her with her shiny blonde hair down and wondered how long it was. "I am sure that your father keeps an eye on you as well?" he asked. "Well, I guess he does, but I do manage quite well on my own," Rebecca stated. She wanted him to know that she was under her father's thumb all the time. "Oh, by the way, my mother loved those pillowcases, and if you are going to be at the market Saturday, I would love to drop by and get some more. My mother's friends all saw them and wanted some as well," Cade said, hoping she was going to say yes! "That is wonderful, I am happy that she was pleased with them, and yes, I will be. In fact, that is what I am doing here. I needed some things to make my bread that I sell. I must be getting back soon, but I have enjoyed running in to you. I am looking forward to seeing you on Saturday." Rebecca knew that she was taking a big chance where anyone could see them, but she did not want to leave. In fact, she would love to stand there all day. However, the risk was too great. She did not want to mess up the chance to be able to see him every week. Rebecca knew her father well, and before he was embarrassed or thought she was considering leaving the community, he would force her to marry Ezekiel. Cade could not stand the thought of her leaving. Was it because she was scared of being caught by someone, or was it because she really did not like him? He knew he would not be able to sleep tonight thinking about her. He really had not been able to do much of anything since he had seen her last Saturday. He could not stop thinking about her. "Cade, did you hear me?" Rebecca asked. She could tell that he was lost in thought and wondered if he could be thinking about her. Cade looked at her with a look of total embarrassment and said, "Oh god! I am sorry, I was thinking about a question I want to ask you before you leave." Rebecca's heart began to beat wildly, and she prayed silently that he would not ask her to go with him somewhere because she knew that she did not have the strength to tell him no. "Yes, what is the question?" she asked as she tried to hold her breath. "Is there any exception to letting a visitor come to observe your lifestyle?" Cade asked. "I am not sure, but you can ask my father Saturday if you wish," Rebecca said as she was turning to leave. Cade could not stand it any longer; he had to take a chance. When she was almost out of arm's reach, he grabbed her arm and said, "I am looking forward to seeing you Saturday, Rebecca." She almost lost her breath. It took her several seconds to be able to speak. She could feel her face hot from his words. There was no mistaking his meaning. He was interested in her, she was sure of it. *Oh! How could this be!* "As I am you, Cade," she replied. When he touched her, it was as if he had branded her. She had never felt that feeling before. As she walked away, she could barely gain her composure. She paid for her groceries and loaded them in her buggy. Her mind was reeling at the possibilities of him being interested in her. She even thought about secretly seeing him if the chance arose. She also could not help dreaming that there might be a future for them.

CHAPTER 2

Rebecca had spent the rest of the week thinking about Cade. She was very anxious to see him today. She was not able to sleep last night for thinking about him and the anticipation of their meeting today. She was readying herself when she heard Amos come through her door. "Becca!" Amos yelled. "Up here, be there in a minute!" she yelled back. When she started down the stairs, Amos was waiting at the bottom for her. "Father sent me here to tell you that John will be going with you today. Father and I are not finished with the planting, and we are going to stay home. John will meet you at the market. I can help you get loaded if you need me to." "No, brother dear, I can do it. I have most of my stuff in there anyway. I could not sleep the past few nights. I decided I'd rather get up and work than to lie there and stare at the ceiling," she said as she laughed softly, rolling her eyes. Amos smiled and walked out the door. Rebecca was elated that her father was not going to be there today. She wanted to be able to talk to Cade without his watchful eye. She grabbed her loaded boxes and loaded them in the wagon. She could not help but be nervous. She wanted to keep his interest although she knew if it progressed into something more, she would eventually have to make a decision about her beliefs. The only thing she wanted to think about now was seeing him today however.

She arrived a little early and began to unload her goods. She had lifted the curtain on the tent only a short while when Cade had pulled up. He sat in his car a while before he had gotten out, and she thought that to be strange. He meandered around the other tents before he came into hers. "Good morning, Rebecca!" he said joyfully. "Good morning to you, Mr. Matthews," Rebecca said. Cade was puzzled by her calling him Mr. Matthews when suddenly it hit him that she was only doing that because others were listening. He walked closer and said, "I thought we had agreed for you to

19

call me Cade?" "I do not want the others to say anything. I will call you that when we are in private if that is okay." Cade could barely believe what he had heard. Private? Was she planning on meeting him privately? His head could not stop processing the possibilities. He had given that some thought himself and was unsure how that could happen although he would do anything to spend some time alone with her. "Rebecca, could we meet privately?" He could not believe he had actually asked her that. "I am sorry if that is improper, but I cannot stop thinking about you. My intentions are strictly harmless, I assure you I only want to talk with you." Rebecca was shocked at his offer. She quickly turned and walked to the row of pillowcases that were hanging in the back of the tent. She had hung them there on purpose to allow her to be able to talk where no one could hear them. Cade followed her, hoping that he had not been too forward and had not offended her. "I will give it some thought, and if you could meet me at the grocery store on Wednesday morning, I will give you my answer." She turned and walked to the far end of the tent and retrieved a set of pillowcases that she had already packaged for him. These were her best work of the week. Cade whispered, "Rebecca, please do think about it. I would love to spend some time with you. You are a beautiful person, and I am intrigued by you. I cannot seem to get you out of my thoughts." Rebecca turned and smiled a smile that could have lit the darkest night and replied, "I cannot stop thinking about you either. I promise to give it some thought as to how we can meet if you are willing to do as it is necessary." Cade was still dazed at the smile she had just given him. He could not believe he was acting like this. How could his feelings be so strong for a person that he had briefly met? He suddenly came back to reality and answered, "I will do whatever I have to, Rebecca!" He paid for the pillowcases and left the tent. He meandered through the other tents as not to look so suspicious and returned to his car. Once again he could not make himself leave. He sat and watched Rebecca for a little while before he finally made himself leave.

 The crowd had dwindled down to just a few, and Rebecca decided to have some lunch. She had been so excited to leave this morning she had only taken the time for coffee. She sat in the back of her tent and began to think of how she could meet Cade. The rest of the day had gone by quickly, and she had sold all of her pillowcases and most of her canned goods. She was pleased at the money she had made. She had waited for John to pack his things in his buggy, and together they headed for home. They were about a mile away from Rebecca's house when she passed a ball field that was off the road a good bit. It suddenly hit her that Cade could park his car after dark one night, and she could ride her horse to see him. She would have to be careful not to gain the attention of anyone, but it was worth the risk. She had unloaded her things and fed her animals, and she was filled with excitement of the prospect of their first private meeting.

She had gotten up the next morning much in the usual way. She decided to see if she could find a path on the back of her property that would afford her some added cover to accomplish her secret meeting. She saddled Daniel's horse and struck out. She had lived here all of her life and knew the land like the back of her hand. She found her way much easier than she had anticipated that it would be. She thought to herself how good this was going to be. She was on her way back when a limb had grabbed her bonnet, pulling it from her head. She decided to let her long hair down and enjoyed the freedom that it suggested. Rebecca had made it to the barn to unsaddle her horse when someone clearing his throat startled her. "Good morning, Rebecca," Ezekiel said in a strange voice. Rebecca realized that her hair was down and quickly worked to put her bonnet back on and tucked her hair under it. "Hello, Ezekiel, I am sorry, I did not know anyone was here. I apologize for you finding me in this condition. I thought that one of my cows had gotten out, and I went to try to find it. A limb removed my bonnet," she explained. Ezekiel looked at her and, with a soft tender voice, said, "There is no need to apologize, Rebecca. I know it is not proper, but I must say how beautiful you look with it down." She was shocked at his response. His statement was in a lot of ways more improper than anything that Cade had said to her. Ezekiel was a pillar of the Amish community and held to the beliefs of the Ordnung and the Amish Church, which put no value in personal appearances. She knew that words like that were probably exchanged between husband and wife, but never should it have been said to her in this situation. Rebecca replied shyly, "Thank you." Ezekiel continued, "Do you need me to help you round it back up?" Rebecca, leading Daniel's horse back in the barn, said, "It was only hiding, it was there all along. Thank you for your kindness however." Ezekiel took the horse's reins from her, letting his hand linger on hers for a brief moment. Rebecca could not help but notice this and immediately moved hers. She was not a cruel person at all; however, she did not want him to read anything into her actions. He unsaddled her horse and returned it to its stall. Rebecca watched as he tidied up the barn and brought more hay from the loft for her. She could not help but think that it was nice to have a man to do all those things for her again. Cade, suddenly creeping back in her thoughts, extinguished any thoughts of Ezekiel. Rebecca knew that there was no chance that Cade would convert to her world nor would he be allowed to. If she were to ask her father to allow it, he would never put it before the bishop for approval. Although she knew that many Amish communities did not practice shunning anymore, their community did. They dealt harshly with those that do not hold the beliefs and practices of the Ordnung. When Ezekiel was finished, she felt that she should at least offer him a glass of lemonade. "Well, that should get you through till Samuel is through with his planting at least," Ezekiel stated as he wiped the sweat from his brow with his handkerchief. "Thank you again for the help, Ezekiel, may I offer you a glass of cold lemonade?" Rebecca asked reluctantly. "Yes, that would be great!" he replied. He followed her back to her house and sat on the porch. It was not allowed for him to enter the house with no one there. He sat in a rocker on the porch and waited patiently on her to return with the lemonade. He drank it thirstily and said, "That was really good, Rebecca, thank you very much. I must get back to pick Mary Grace up from her grandmother's. Please call on me if you need me." Rebecca watched as he pulled away and once again relived the look on his face when he saw her with her hair down. He probably would make a good husband, and one thing was sure. She saw more passion in that one look than she saw out of Daniel the whole time they were married; however, it was nothing compared to the feeling she felt when Cade had touched her. As soon as she thought about it, her blood ran hot in her veins. She could not wait till Wednesday to meet him.

Rebecca busied herself to make the time pass quickly. She awakened Wednesday morning bright and early at the prospect of seeing Cade. She finished with her chores and went upstairs to freshen up. When she returned downstairs, Sarah had let herself in and was waiting in the kitchen. "Sarah! You scared me. What are you doing here?" Rebecca asked in worried voice. "Mother is not feeling well, and with Father and John and David still planting, she was wondering if you could go to the store for her. She also wants you to bring Annie back home with you if you can," Sarah said as she handed her a list and money. "Sure, tell Mother that I will go now. I had planned to go anyway. Come with me and I will drop you off at the driveway." Rebecca hitched the horse and buggy and made her way to her parents' drive. When she had dropped Sarah off, she could see her father and brothers in the field and waved as she passed. When she was close to the grocery store, her heart began to race. She surveyed the parking lot for Cade's car, and when she spotted it, she felt like she had butterflies in her stomach. She grabbed her purse and headed in. She started filling her cart as usual. She did not want it to look as though she had come only to see

Cade. When she rounded the aisle, he was standing there, pretending to look at all the coffees. "Hello, Rebecca, how are you?" Cade asked. "I am very well, thank you for asking. I see that you ran out of coffee again," she stated with a devilish grin. "No, actually not this time, I was just waiting for you, Bec," he said in a whispered voice. She could not believe he called her that. Her face suddenly became very hot! Cade watched as she blushed. This thrilled him beyond reason. He had not seen a woman do that in a long time. "I have missed you terribly. I know that sounds corny, but it's true," he explained. Rebecca had never felt like this before, she was fighting with her emotions, she had this sudden urge to kiss him. "Have you given any thought to our meeting?" Cade asked anxiously. "Yes, I have, if you would like, we can meet tomorrow night. I have made you a map, quickly look at it and tell me if you know where this is at," she whispered. Cade took the map from her, and his hands began to tremble. He surveyed the map and said, "Yes, I can find this. What time do you want to meet?" She spotted a neighbor coming in the door, she pretended to look at the coffee and whispered, "Ten, is that okay?" Cade could not believe she was even asking that. He would meet her tonight on the moon if that is what she wanted. "Yes, absolutely, that is great!" he said as she turned to walk away. He was so excited he left the store feeling as though he was walking on air.

CHAPTER 3

Rebecca brought Annie home the next day and checked on her mother, who was feeling better. She told her that she was going back home to bake and was going to bed early. She wanted her to know this so no one would bother her anymore today. When she started home, she could hardly keep herself on the seat. Was she really doing this? Could she possibly get away with it? She was both nervous and excited. When she returned home, she finished her chores that had to be done and went upstairs to bath. She lingered a long while in the tub of warm water. She had purchased some sweet-smelling shampoo from the grocery store the day before and began to wash her long hair. This was forbidden of course, and when she returned home, she would have to bath with the homemade soap that she normally used. She was about through when she decided that she would get one of Daniel's razors and attempt to shave her legs. She did not anticipate Cade seeing them; however, she had wanted to do that for a while. Women of the Amish community were not allowed to shave unwanted body hair or to cut their hair at all. She carefully shaved her legs and underarms. She loved the feeling of how smooth and soft they were. She crawled from the tub and made sure she had washed the tub properly so no one would know. That was the last thing she needed—Sarah or Katie coming to stay and seeing that. She knew without a doubt they would go straight to her mother with it. She put on her skirt and blouse and decided to leave her apron off. She tucked her blouse in loosely; she did not want to accentuate her full bosom too much. Rebecca once again retrieved her mirror and brushed her beautiful long hair. She pulled it back from her face, leaving it to fall where it pleased. She had been so busy dressing she had not noticed that it had began to get dark, and she would need to light the candles soon. She had eaten breakfast with Annie this morning but could not force herself to eat anything else. The butterflies she had would not allow it. As she sat in the living room, she made a plan of what to do. She would leave her lamp in the barn until she returned. Once she was safe inside the barn, she could easily find her way back to her bed without the assistance of a lantern. She waited nervously until the huge grandfather clock in the foyer struck nine. She was not sure how long it would take her to get to the ball field in the dark, so she decided to leave. She blew the last of the lanterns out and ran quietly to the barn. She placed the saddle on Daniel's horse and led it to the barn door. She thought to herself, *Well, are you really going to do this?* She peeked out the barn door one last time to make sure she saw no one on the road, and led her horse outside. She climbed in the saddle and, as quietly as she could, rode away. When she had reached the spot where she was sure she was out of sight, she urged the horse faster. It was a full moon, and everything was glistening in the light of the moon. When she had went as far as she could go on the horse, she tied him to a tree and proceeded on foot. When she came out of the woods, her heart skipped a beat when she saw Cade standing there. He had gotten there early in his haste to see her. He heard something in the bushes and turned to see if it was Rebecca. When he saw her, he could not believe his eyes. She was the most beautiful woman she had ever seen. Her hair was down to her waist and was pulled away from her face so that even in the moonlight, you could see those crystal blue eyes. He let out a breath, and as she got closer, he saw that she was not in full Amish dress. He admired her womanly curves and tried to wipe any disrespectful thought from his mind. Rebecca was, despite her being a widow, a very innocent woman whom he wanted to, strangely enough, never be away from. He had told himself all day that he was to stay in control at all times tonight; however, seeing her, he wondered if he could do that. When she was near him, she motioned for him to follow her. She led him to a place where if someone pulled in, they would be hidden. "Hey, how are you?" Cade asked quietly. "Well, if you must know, I am scared to death!" she responded. Cade, without thinking, put his hand on her back as a sign of reassurance and said, "I know, I am sorry that I made you do this." Rebecca tried to compose herself, but she knew he saw the look on her face. Cade could not help it; he slowly kissed her lips as she sat there without moving anything at first. When he opened his eyes and saw her staring at him with passion-filled flames flickering in those blue eyes, he very gently put his hands on each side of her face and tenderly yet passionately kissed her beautiful full lips. Rebecca began to kiss him back. Only this time, she kissed him like she had done in her dreams. She was shocked at her behavior; she could not believe the feeling that had come over her. She was sure that she had just melted right there into a puddle of mud. The realization of what was happening hit her like a bolt of lightning. She pushed away from him with force. Cade could see that it was too much too fast for her. He thought she was going to leave. He was so mad at himself for not having control. He was fixing to blow this, and he would never be able to forgive himself. "Bec, I am sorry! I promise you that I had no intentions of doing that. It's . . . It's just, well, when I saw how beautiful you were, I kinda lost it. I am not here because I only want to sleep with you." Rebecca, suddenly feeling unsure about her decision, began to walk back where her horse was tied. Cade ran behind her; when he was close to her, he jumped in front of her. He could see that she had tears streaming down her face. "Oh god! Bec, I am sorry! Please hear me out. I think I am in love with you." The words stopped Rebecca in her tracks. She stood there looking at him as though she had been hit with a club. Cade continued as he ran his hands through his long black hair. "Ever since the first time I laid eyes on you, I have not been able to get you off my mind. I told myself how stupid that was a million times. I even told myself that you would never have someone like me. I told myself that we were from different worlds, but none of that worked." He walked to her and very gently put his hand on her cheek. She could tell that he meant what he was saying. She knew she was naive in many ways, but she did not think that anyone could fake being that sincere. He wiped the tears from her face and said, "Rebecca, I love you, baby." He waited to see her reaction, and when she flew into his arms, he felt like a mountain had been removed from his shoulders. He held her for a moment; then she once again pulled herself from him so she could look into his eyes. "I am in love with you as well, Cade. I have also told myself how stupid I was, and I have thought about all that I will have to endure for us to be together. I must be honest because without it, I am nothing." Cade's heart sank; he knew what she was saying. If she chose a life with him, she would never see her family again. He asked her, "What would I have to do to join the Amish Church?" Rebecca could not believe her ears. Surely he was not serious about converting to her way of life. "Cade, you would not like it. I am Amish, and I don't like it." "Well, there is our answer then. If you are unhappy, leave with me right now. I know you don't know that much about me, but I assure you that I will make a good husband, and I want kids. I have money, Rebecca, I will take care of you!" Rebecca put her fingers over his mouth and caressed his handsome face. Even touching him gently drove her crazy. He had given this some thought it seems, and that she was appreciative of; however, there were things they needed to know about each other before they just ran off together. "Cade, there are things that you need to know about me," she said reluctantly. "What, do you have kids already? Great! I don't care," Cade asked. Rebecca laughed and said, "No, I do not have any children. Don't you think we need to slow down just a bit and make sure this is what we both want? I mean, for you, it would be easy, but for me, it is going to be a huge change. This is not a decision that we should make tonight. I am not saying no at all. I am just saying that we need to think about this some more." Cade shook his head in agreement and put his arms around her tiny waist. He noticed how full her breast was, and he ached to kiss her again. He hugged her tight to him, and he loved how her hair fell around his face. "Okay, we will take some time to get to know one another better, but I want you to know that if you should get caught seeing me and you have to leave, I will marry you and take care of you forever." He kissed her lips with such tenderness that it made her dizzy. She did not want to leave him ever; however, she wanted to be sure of her decision. When he released her, she took him by the hand and led them to a place where they could sit and talk. "So tell me about your family, Bec," Cade asked. "Well, there are nine of us altogether. I have three other sisters and five brothers. David is the oldest, and he plans on getting married this winter." "How is it that you married first?" Cade asked. "Well, I was the first to finish my rumspringa and decided to commit to the Ordnung and the Amish Church," she replied. "Did you love your husband?" Cade asked. "No, I did not, we were more like brother and sister than husband and wife. That is something that you need to know as well. I am very inexperienced when it comes to being intimate with a man," she explained shyly. "I never felt anything for Daniel at all. I hated my life and was ashamed that I had been so stupid as to marry a man that I did not love. My mother told me that was all that she felt for my father when they married. She also said that the intimate part did not matter because that is only necessary to have children. Sex in my world is not like that in yours." Cade listened to her intently; when she had finished, he said, "Bec, there's only so much I can do to keep my hands off you right now. My body is aching for you at this moment. I have tried to keep any impure thought from my mind, but you are an incredibly beautiful woman. However, I am pleased that you have not slept around. I find that most attractive about you. I have not dated that much, and I have only slept with a couple of women myself. One reason I have not found anyone that I could get serious about was because . . . well, I am not sure how to say this, so I will just come right out and say it. I am a wealthy man, Bec, and women only want me to shower them with material things. They do not have any morals or integrity. I was not going to lower my standards just to say I have a wife. I do not want a trophy wife. I want a wife that will always be there with me with or without my money. I love your innocence, and I think when the time is right, we will be great together. If it is anything like that kiss a few minutes ago, it will be awesome!" Cade said too loudly. Rebecca reminded him to keep it down, laughing the whole time. "I'm sorry," he said. "I think you are incredibly sexy, and there is nothing I would like better than to make love to you right now. I also know that I would be doing you harm if I do that. When you have injured someone's soul, there is no repairing it," Cade explained. They sat for hours and talked about the way they felt and things they wanted out of life. Cade was extremely touched at how sincere and honest she was. He could not bear the thought of having to be without her. They talked all night and giving no thought as to what time it was. It was when she heard a rooster from a nearby farm crow that she realized the time. "Oh no, I must go now, my brother is going to be there early this morning to help me plant," Rebecca said as she got up quickly, dusting off her dress. Cade stood to his feet and asked, "When will I be able to see you again?" Rebecca quickly thought and answered, "I have lots of things to prepare for the market Saturday. I must get them ready." "Bec, if it is money that you need, I will be more than happy to—" She once again put her finger over his mouth and replied, "I enjoy it, and it is what is expected of me. After all, I am a widow. Thank you very much, that is very sweet of you." He took her into his arms and held her close for a moment and then, filling his fingers with her long beautiful hair, kissed her sweetly. The tenderness rendered her speechless and dizzy. She gathered her composure and said, "Will you come to the market Saturday?" "Yes, of course, I will be there!" he quickly replied. "If my father is there, I will not be able to talk as before. If I cannot, I will put a note in your bag," she said as she started to run in the direction of her horse. Cade followed her and watched as she mounted Daniel's horse. She blew him a kiss and reined the horse toward her house. Cade was amazed at her beauty. He could not wait to see her again.

CHAPTER 4

Rebecca had made it home and changed her clothes. She once again put her normal Amish attire on, complete with bonnet. She was in the kitchen when John made it there. He thought it strange that she was so awake and chipper this morning. She was not a morning person and had been sluggish every time he had seen her lately. "What has got you in such good spirits, sister dear?" he asked with a smirk. "Oh, nothing, nothing at all. I got some things that I was worried about settled last night. Maybe that is why." She could not believe she had just told a half lie to her brother. She had never really been good at it, and she tried not to make eye contact. John was a year younger than she, and he had only recently finished rumspringa and committed to the Ordnung. He had a fling or two while he was doing his running around. Although he had not said it, she was sure he had even lost his virginity. He was very handsome, and even the Amish girls his age were trying to get his attention. He had not yet chosen a mate however. He said he wanted to wait a little longer. He continued to look at her strangely, and she felt really uncomfortable. "Becca, you know you can talk to me, right? I will not judge you at all. I am trustworthy, and I have never been a tattletale. I have done things that I am not proud of, and there is nothing I can do about that. I have asked for forgiveness, and I am ready start fresh. But I would never pass judgment on you. Please know that!" Rebecca knew he was telling the truth. She had always been able to talk to him. She had held it in all she could. "Brother, I have met someone," she blurted out. John was not surprised at all. "Ezekiel, right?" he asked with a devilish look. "No, this man is from the English world. I met him at the market a couple weeks ago, and I am madly in love!" she yelled. "A couple of weeks and you're already madly in love?" he said as if she had lost her mind. "I would not try to dampen your spirit for nothing. If you are sure that is what you want to pursue, then so be it, but I feel that I would not be doing you justice if I did not warn you that the English men think we are freaks. They think that they can talk their way into your skirt. They are looking for one thing and one only." "John, Cade is not like that!" she retorted. "How do you know this? Have you talked with him long enough to find this out?" he asked firmly. "Yes, as a matter of fact, I have last night. I met him, and we talked all night long. He told me how he felt about me. He is in love with me too. He wants to marry me. In fact, he wanted me to leave with him last night. When I explained to him what I would be leaving, he wanted to know if he could convert to my world. He is very sincere, John, I am *not* that naive, brother. I think I could tell if he were only interested in sleeping with me," she said adamantly. "Okay, okay, I get it! If you think that he is honest in his intentions and you truly love him, then pursue it if that is what you want. All I ask is that you think about it a lot before you act, and most of all, you better let me know before you run off!" he said with a smile. John got up and gave his sister a hug. "I love you, sister, no matter what. If you choose this, I will still love you." He picked his hat up and walked out of the kitchen. She was not sorry that she had told him. She needed someone to talk to about this. John was very wise for his age, and his experience had left him wiser no doubt, but she suspected a little bitterness. He had never really talked about it, but now more than ever, she suspected that he too had fallen in love with someone from the English world. However, unlike her, his feelings were not returned. She hoped they would have more time to talk about this. Rebecca put her cup in the sink and started her chores. She gathered her planting sack and headed off to the field to help John. "How is Mother today?" she asked, to help change the subject. "She is better although I do think she is pregnant again," John said with worry. Rebecca lost her balance. "Oh, John, this is not good. You know what happened with Annie—" John interrupted her, "Yes, I know all too well. I just hope if she is, the Lord will have mercy on her." Rebecca could not believe that her mother could be pregnant again. She had nearly died when Annie was born. The doctor who delivered Annie told her never to get pregnant again. He suggested sterilization, but they would not hear of it. Rebecca was lost in thought; she was almost through with her row of potatoes when John asked unexpectedly, "Did you sleep with him, Becca?" Rebecca looked at him with a look that told him of his crudeness. "I am sorry if I am prying, but I cannot help it. The idea has been eating at me all day, but there is no need to answer, I know you well enough to read your face. You didn't." Rebecca was shocked at the question and was embarrassed that he would think she had on the first time of seeing him. Although, after she thought about it, it did seem strange that they professed their undying love for one another after only knowing each other so briefly. "John, tell me what happened between you and the English girl. I know it hurt you deeply. You still carry this bitterness in your heart," Rebecca stated. "I knew I loved her the first time we met. She was so beautiful and easy to talk to. We just hit it off! I wanted to marry her and renounce my Amish heritage. We slept together for a while. She discovered a month later that she was pregnant. I was so excited! I went and bartered for a ring and had planned to ask her to marry me when I found out that I was not the only guy she had been sleeping with. Needless to say, I never saw her again." "John, what if the baby was yours! Did you ever find out?" Rebecca exclaimed. "No, and I try not to think about it. I don't want to put myself in that situation anymore, that is why I made my commitment to the Ordnung. It will never let you down or leave you." Rebecca rushed over to her brother and hugged him tightly. They both were crying like children. "John, surely you do not care if you have a child out there somewhere. What if she gave it away or is mistreating it? Please, you have to find out!" she cried. John wiped his face and continued with his planting. Rebecca gave him his space and knew he was thinking. By midafternoon, they were finished, and Rebecca was exhausted. She had been running on adrenaline, but after a while, even it gave out. John still had not said anything else on the matter, and when she had invited him for refreshments, he shook his head no and continued home. She knew when he was ready to talk about it; again, she would let him bring it up. There was only a certain amount of hurt a person could take. She also knew why he had been so protective of her about Cade. He still thought somewhere in the back of his mind that Cade was lying and had planned to do her the same way. She thought about all that he said, and she was beginning to have doubts. She considered John to be very wise, and if this girl fooled him, then surely Cade was capable of fooling her. She would set some traps and just see. She would plan to meet him again and offer herself to him. She knew she would never go through with it. This would be just to get his reaction of course. She took a warm bath and called it a night. The next morning, she was up with the roosters and had baked all day long. She only had doillies to sell as she had sold all of her embroidered pillowcases the week before. She wanted to make time to go see her mother. She wanted to ask her herself if she was in fact going to have another child. She gathered up her sewing goods and then decided she had enough time for a quick visit to her mother's. When she arrived, she found her mother in the kitchen preparing her supper in the usual fashion. Annie had greeted her with smiles and a great big hug as usual.

Sarah and Katie were both helping their mother prepare their meal, and all were glad to see her. She fixed herself a glass of mint tea and sat at the table. Her mother was much like John, she could tell when something was on your mind and immediately asked, "Is everything all right, Becca?" Rebecca smiled and said, "Yes, is everything okay with you?" Mary Fisher was a very kind woman. In all of Rebecca's years at home, she had never heard her mother say an unkind word. Rebecca's mother was, above all else, honest and if you ask her a question, she would answer it. "Mother, may I speak with you in private?" Mary motioned for the girls to leave them. When they were all alone, Rebecca asked, "Mother, are you expecting again?" Mary never changed her expression and answered, "Yes, I am, Becca." Rebecca did not know whether to be angry or elated. She took a deep breath and said, "Are you sure this is a good idea?" Mary just chuckled and said, "Well, Rebecca, that I am not sure, but there is nothing I can do about it now, is there? This is as much a surprise to your father and me as it is to you. We had not planned on this at all. However, God knows what is best for us, and I have faith that he will see us through it whatever the outcome is to be." Rebecca loved her mother dearly and went over and knelt beside her and laid her head on her lap. "I love you, Mother!" Rebecca said as her eyes welled with tears. Mary pulled her daughter's face up so that she could look into those beautiful blue eyes and said, "I will not have you worrying over this. Whatever happens, this is a gift from God. I do not regret it at all." Rebecca shook her head in agreement and asked, "When are you going to tell everyone?" "Actually, we are not going to say anything for a little while yet. I am planning to go to the doctor next week, and I would love it if you came along," Mary stated. Rebecca quickly replied, "I would love to." It was getting dark, so Rebecca decided to make her way home. She had made it to her buggy when John came running out of the house. "Becca, can I stay with you tonight?" he asked as though something were chasing him. "Yes, of course, you may, John," she answered. He already had his clothes in a satchel, which he had thrown over his shoulder. John threw it in the buggy and hopped in the seat. When they had traveled to the end of the drive, Rebecca could not hold it any longer. "What is the matter, John?" John looked down at his feet and said, "I have decided to find out, and I need your help. You are the only link I have to the outside world." Rebecca thought a minute and knew she could count on Cade's help. She remained silent till they had unhitched her horse and made it into the house. She lit the lanterns and went to the kitchen to prepare them something to eat. When John came inside, he had finished attending to the livestock, and Rebecca had supper prepared. She was already seated at the table with a pen and some stationery. After John had extended the evening prayer, Rebecca asked, "I am sure that Cade will help, but do I have your permission to tell him what this is about?" John, not hesitating, said, "Yes, absolutely. I want him to know how serious this is. I also want him to know that you told me about the two of you. I want to make him accountable for his treatment of you. I am sorry that I said the things that I said. It is very unfair for me to judge him for the actions of another. He may have only the highest intentions for you, and for your sake, I hope so. I will not lie for you, but you have my word that I will tell no one." Rebecca thanked him for his kind words, and John began to tell her all he knew about his affair. "Her name is Kelly Douglas, she should be nineteen now, and her birthday is February 13." He went on to tell the last address to where she lived and all the information he could remember. They sat and talked a while about all of the possibilities of finding out the truth of whether he had a child or not. When they had talked the subject to death, they decided to turn in.

Rebecca was dressed and had breakfast ready when John finished up with the chores. He loaded her buggy, and after they ate, they rode for town. When they had come to the driveway of her parents', Amos was waiting there and said, "John, Father wants you to go to the market today. Mother is still not feeling well, and he is gonna stay with her today." John hopped down from his wagon and grabbed the reins of his father's buggy. Amos watched as the two buggies were out of sight. When they reached the market, Rebecca surveyed the parking lot to make sure that Cade was not already there. She did not see his car and pulled her buggy up to the back of the tent. She quickly unloaded her goods and opened up her curtain. The day started out busier than most, and before she knew it, lunchtime had arrived. She tried not to let it show, but she was getting more and more upset. Maybe John was right. Maybe all Cade wanted was to sleep with her, and when she would not, he decided it was not worth the effort. John knew his sister well, and he could see by her body language that she was upset. She had gone to the back of the tent to retrieve some more loaves of bread to put out when Cade had pulled in the parking lot. She had seen him and was startled to see him when he walked up. "Good day, Mr. Matthews, what can I help you with today?" Rebecca said, barely smiling. Cade wondered if he had offended her the other night or maybe she was upset because he was so late. He said, "Good day to you, Rebecca. Do you have any more of those pillowcases that I bought last week?" Rebecca walked to the back of the tent to pretend to look. "Bec, I am sorry I am late. I had a business meeting that ran long, and I have a surprise for you. Can we please meet tonight? I am about to burst with excitement." Rebecca was relieved when she heard the urgency in his voice. She knew then that the feelings he had for her had not changed. The crowd had dwindled a little, and Rebecca called John over to them. She knew that now that John knew her secret that she could talk longer without suspicion if he were standing there too. Rebecca said in a low voice, "Cade, this is John, my brother. I hope that you are not upset, but I told him about us. I need to ask a favor of you too. There is a note in the bag that I am going to give you. When you get to your car, would you read it before you leave and let me know if you think you can do it?" Cade answered, "Yes, of course. Is everything all right, Bec?" She shook her head and smiled as one of the women from the other tent came up to them. "Excuse me but, John, could I borrow you for a moment. I need you to load this furniture for me if you would," Mrs. King asked. John smiled and left with her. Cade continued, "Well, if you do not have any more of the pillowcases, give me four loaves of that bread then." Rebecca grabbed the bread and went to the back of the store to bag it. "Yes, I will meet you tonight, same place and time." Cade smiled; he could not wait to tell Rebecca what he had done. He hoped she would love the idea as much as he did. He took the bag and did as he was asked. When he reached his car, he read the note:

My dearest Cade,

    My brother John met an English girl during his rumspringa and fell in love. He then learned that the love he felt for her was not returned. She was also seeing another man. A short time later, she learned that she was pregnant. John does not know whether the child is his or not, but wishes to find out. If you could, would you please see if you could find this person for us.

He went on to read the rest of the note. He especially loved the way she signed it. "I love you, Bec." He read that line over and over. He was not sure how to tell her that he would help them in their endeavor, so he decided to go back to her tent under the pretense of buying something else. Cade had arrived back under her tent and found Rebecca was in the back in a curtained room for her privacy. Cade called her name as he entered. She was startled to see him there and sucked in her breath. He looked around to see if anyone was near and grabbed her and pulled her to him. He kissed those full red lips passionately and released her quickly. Rebecca was addled over what had just occurred, but she loved it! She smiled at him with a devilish grin while she straightened her bonnet. "Sorry to bother you again, Rebecca, but I decided to buy those lace doilies after all." Rebecca smiled at him and replied, "How many would you like, Mr. Matthews?" "Well, why don't you just give me all of them?" Cade replied. Rebecca was shocked. She gave him a look of total bewilderment and whispered, "Cade, you do not have to do that." He smiled at her and said, "Did you hear what I said, Mrs. Matthews?" Rebecca's face turned as red as beet juice. She hoped that no one had heard him, but it did sound so good! She retrieved all the doilies and bagged them. When Cade started to leave, he whispered, "I would love to help find this person for John. I will let you know something as soon as I can." Cade returned to his car. When he had gone, Rebecca played what he had said over and over in her mind. She did love him, and she was most positive that she wanted to spend the rest of her life with him. The only thing she was not ready to do was give up her family. She had sold almost everything and was loading her empty boxes up when Mrs. King walked over. "We sure had a good day, didn't we?" Rebecca smiled and said, "Yes, we did!" "Where is Samuel today, Rebecca?" Mrs. King asked. "My mother is not feeling well, and he stayed home to see to her today," Rebecca replied. "Well, tell Mary that I hope she is feeling better soon and I will try to get by there this week some time." Rebecca smiled and nodded her head. She had cleaned her tent and loaded her things long before John had finished his. When he decided to leave, she helped load his as well. She reined her horse home with the excitement of meeting Cade tonight. When she arrived home, she unhitched her horse and fed him. She hoped that he would be rested in time to bring her to meet her sweet Cade tonight. She carried her things in and went upstairs to bath. Rebecca could not wait to see Cade again. Her wanting to be with him all the time was becoming greater and greater. She knew that her decision time was getting closer. She dried herself and put on the same clothes that she had worn before. She put her hair in a ponytail that hung long on one side with a satin ribbon holding it. She waited till the clock struck nine, and she started on her way. She had tied her horse in the same way she had before and walked into view. Cade was standing there waiting for her. He grabbed her sweetly and held her close. He kissed her on the forehead and said, "I cannot stand being away from you any longer." He caressed her face in his hands while he looked deeply into those crystal blue eyes. "I love you, Rebecca, and it is a strong and undying love." Cade got down on one knee and pulled a ring from his pocket and said, "Rebecca, will you marry me?" She was speechless; her eyes filled with tears as he slipped the beautiful ring on her finger. She had never had any jewelry before, but this had to be the most beautiful thing she had ever seen. "Cade, are you sure this is what you want?" Rebecca asked. He replied, "I have never been surer of anything in my life, Bec." He got up off his knee, and Rebecca kissed him tenderly. "Yes, Cade, I will marry you," she whispered. Cade's excitement was hard to control. He wanted so badly to make love to her at this very moment. He knew that was a natural thing for two people to do. She grabbed his hand and led him to a place where they could sit. "Rebecca, this is a blue diamond. I chose it so that you could see how very beautiful your eyes are. It reminded me of your eyes. This is not all I bought today. Rebecca, I bought us a house. It is a farm with lots of land to do with however you want. There is plenty of it for our kids to play in as well. Never have I wanted anything as bad as I want to spend the rest of my life with you." He kissed her tenderly at first. When she was meeting his lips and looking into his eyes, he knew that she was not frightened of him anymore. He slowly began to search her mouth with his tongue. He held her close while keeping his hands from any body part that would suggest that he was expecting more. Rebecca kissed him in a more passionate way than she had ever kissed anyone in her life. She put her hand on his chest as he kissed her face and started for her neck. He suddenly decided that he should be the one to stop this before it led to her being upset again. "Bec, there is nothing I want any more than to make love to you right now. My body aches for you when I am near you and begs for you when I am away from you. But I am not going to let our first time be on the ground either." Rebecca covered his mouth with a kiss that told him of her need for him. As she stood, she said, "Well, let us go to my bed then." Cade could not believe his ears. He wanted this woman so badly, but he was not taking a chance that she would regret her decision in the morning. "Bec, are you sure this is what you want?" When she turned to look at him, her eyes conveyed the need for him. His body ached at the thought of lying next to her, making passionate love to the beautiful woman that he loves so dearly. She led him to Daniel's horse that she had tied. He was not a stranger to horses. He had ridden often and was very comfortable. He mounted it first and then pulled her petite body up behind him. Rebecca pointed in the direction they should go. They rode in silence, but with her hands around his waist and his hand resting on hers, their bodies told of their excitement. He could feel her full bosom as it bounced on his back, and it was driving him crazy. When Cade caught a glimpse of a barn, he whispered, "Is this your place?" Rebecca answered back, "Yes. We will take the horse to the barn." When they were at the door of the barn, Rebecca jumped off and opened the door. As Cade shut the door, she lit a lantern so they could see to the horse. Cade very skillfully unsaddled him and put him in his stall where he already had hay and water. As they reached the door to the barn, Cade turned to her and asked, "This is your last chance to back out." Rebecca shook her head no and kissed him tenderly again. She knew that he did not just want sex. He had tried to talk her out of it, and she thought him to be very sincere. They got to the door of the house, and Rebecca made sure that no one was inside; she motioned for Cade to come inside. She lit a small candle that would afford them enough light that they may make their way upstairs. Cade followed behind her as she made her way to her bedroom. Once they were inside, she shut and locked the door. Cade watched as Rebecca closed the wood shutters on the windows. She sat the lit candle on the wick of another and sat the other candles down in holders on each side of the room. When Cade came to her, she took the ribbon from her hair and let it fall freely. Cade took his jacket off and laid it in a chair by the bed. When he turned back to her, he took her into his arms and was determined to make her his. He kissed her lips passionately yet tenderly until both their bodies were on fire. He began to rub her body, conveying his need. She stepped away from him briefly and began to remove her blouse. He watched as she let it rest on her bare shoulders. Her face was flushed, and he knew that she was feeling a little uneasy. "Rebecca, please don't be nervous about me seeing your body. You are a beautiful woman," he said as he placed small kisses on her shoulders. "I have never shown my body to another man before," she whispered. Cade once again looked into her eyes with bewilderment. He was not going to bring Daniel into their lovemaking, but he knew what she meant. When she let her shirt fall to the floor, Cade pushed her hair to one side. He kissed her shoulders and down to the top of her breast that was not covered by her corset. He watched as she undid the corset bra and it was on the floor. Cade grabbed her to him, pulling her hair gently back to allow him access to her neck and chest. He admired her beauty as he kissed his way down to the beautiful mounds that waited for his attention. Rebecca threw her head back and wrapped her arms tightly around him. Her body was on fire and cried for more. Cade pushed her back for a moment and removed his own shirt, when he once again pulled her to him, it was skin on skin. He could feel her full breast as they crushed up against his matted chest. He grabbed a handful of hair and said huskily, "My god, you are beautiful, I love you,

Rebecca!" He kissed her feverishly, and she whimpered as he was commanding her body to move in ways it had never done. He intertwined his fingers in hers and pulled them to her back. When the position she was in made her full bosom push forward, he captured one of the rosy buds and began to suckle it. Rebecca gasped as it sent her body into shock. She knew that lovemaking was supposed to be more than what she and Daniel had done, but never in her wildest dreams did she expect this. Cade had very carefully undone the pin in her skirt. It fell to the floor, and he could not help but stare at her beautiful curves. He looked into her eyes that were half shut with passion and said, "You are the most sensual, beautiful woman I have ever seen, and you are mine!" Cade began to feel the curve of her hips. He squeezed her hips as they were writhing in ecstasy. He lifted her from her clothes that lay in a puddle on the floor and carried her to the bed. He watched as her beautiful body lay out before him. He saw that despite her petiteness was a very voluptuous woman. Her long hair was crumpled all over her pillow. He loved her full red lips that were parted with passion. He watched as her full breast rose and fell with her labored breathing. Her waist was very small, and it led to full hips that were perfectly round. He also saw the dark matted spot that led to that secret place that he wanted to explore. Cade took a moment and removed his shoes. He began removing his pants when he saw her gaze go downward. Rebecca admired his very muscular body. His chest was matted with black hair, and his stomach tight and hard. As his pants were pushed lower, she got her first glimpse of manhood. She bit her bottom lip as it sprang from his pants. She had never seen a man's before, and she thought it to be beautiful. It was pulsating with every heartbeat. Cade lay beside her, and she traced the matted hair on his chest. Cade kissed her lips with hot, wet kisses that did not stop there. He kissed her neck as he whispered, "I love you, baby." He looked into her eyes once more. He wanted to make sure that what he was about to do did not offend her. He positioned himself between her legs and kissed her stomach that were left with flaming kisses. It was when he dared to go lower that he looked at her for her approval. She cupped his face in her hand. She carefully traced his lip with her small finger. When he resumed, he kissed the dark matted place that lay so beautifully under him. When his tongue reached the spot where he knew gave a woman the most pleasure, Rebecca let out a cry. She filled her hands with the bedsheet they were lying on. Her hips rocked back and forth as he pleasured her. Her body was on fire, never had she felt this way before. Something was happening to her, and the pleasure was unreal. She lost the fight to the sensation that had overtaken her, and when she met her release for the very first time, she whispered, "Cade, I love you!" He watched as her body quivered with pleasure. It was when she had suddenly gone very still that he knew she had been satisfied for the moment. Cade lifted himself to hold her tightly. He knew that was the first time for her, and he hoped that he had made it all it could be. Rebecca rubbed his back and buttocks. She was looking into his eyes when she dared to touch it. "Oh!" she exclaimed. As she stroked the long hard member, it became wet with anticipation. Rebecca could not believe herself. She was amazed at how comfortable she felt with him. She wanted to pleasure him beyond pleasure, and he was not expecting what happened next. She positioned herself on top of him. She began kissing his matted chest. She licked his tiny peaks that were nestled there. As she kissed him, her full chest danced under her, exciting him greatly. When she had reached his stomach, she began to trace the trail that led to his manhood with her tongue. Cade's eyes widened at the realization of what she was going to do. It was when she slid his throbbing manhood between those full red lips that Cade's body shook violently. He knew he wanted more of her, and at this rate, he would not last much longer. He grabbed her tiny waist and laid her beneath him. He caressed her face and kissed her lips tenderly. "Mmmmm, baby, you are a wonderful lover," he said with a breathless voice. He began searching that womanly spot that he had tasted only moments ago. Rebecca spread her legs to allow him to explore more fully. When he found it, he teased the pleasure bud with his finger. When he was sure she was ready, he mounted her. Cade entered her with a firm thrust that sent her body soaring. He held her tightly up against him, and he delivered thrust after thrust. "My god, baby, you feel so good. I love making love to you," Cade said with clenched teeth. Rebecca knew that his pleasure was building. His body was on fire as well. Cade's thrusts began harder and faster until they both exploded into tingling pleasure. Cade moaned as he spilled his seed into her. Rebecca gasped as her body was trembling with delight. Cade lay beside her and held her, kissing her nose and face as he said, "Baby, I love you! I want you with me all the time. I want you in my bed where I can pleasure you whenever you like. My heart is so full right now. My god, I cannot get enough of you!" Rebecca smiled at his rambling. She knew just how he felt because she was feeling them too. "I know how you feel, my darling, it is like we were made for one another. I cannot imagine being any more satisfied than at this moment. You are the wonderful lover." Cade squeezed her tight up against him. He wanted this night to last forever. They had lain sharing small talk for a while, just enjoying being in one another's arms when Cade said, "When are we going to be together?" Rebecca lifted her left hand so she could see the ring that was on her finger. It was stunning, and the blue diamond sparkled in the candlelight. "Cade, my mother is expecting again, and the doctor told her when my sister was born that another pregnancy would kill her. I am scared that if I leave right away that the stress will harm her or the baby. I want to be with you more than anything in this world and soon! Is it too much to ask that you give me a little more time?" He brushed the hair from her face and replied, "No, honey, I understand, that would be a tough spot to be in. You know where babies come from, right?" Rebecca smiled. She knew what he was saying, and it was something to think about. She knew well where babies came from, and the fact was that if she were pregnant with his child, she would not regret it. "Cade, I would love to have your children. No matter what happens, I do not regret tonight. I love you so much!" Cade thought about the possibility of her being pregnant and silently cursed himself for not being prepared. He did not want her to have his child out of wedlock. He wanted children with her, but he wanted to wait until she was his. "Speaking of kids, I found that girl that John wanted me to find. She is still living at that address. I had one of my people look into it for me, and I think you should know the girl had twins." Cade got up and took an envelope from his coat pocket. "I have pictures of her and the babies." If she had not been so excited about the pictures and the news, she would have taken him again on the floor. He was a very sexy man. The sight of him fully naked sent chills up her spine again. When she saw the pictures, she knew the babies were John's. They looked just like him. "Oh!" she exclaimed. "Yes, I know, I had the same reaction, they look just like your brother," he explained. "How were you able to do this that fast?" she asked. "I will give you anything you want for the rest of your life, my love," he said as he kissed her once again, laying her under him. He made love to her once more, and it left both of them wondering how they could not be together from this moment on. When they returned to Cade's car, his heart was heavy. He did not want to leave her. He knew the moment that he had kissed her goodbye that this woman was everything to him. If he had to travel to the depths of hell to fight the devil himself, he *would* have her.

Rebecca traveled back home that night deeply troubled. It had been confirmed to her after their lovemaking that Cade was the man for her. Even now, she could still feel the heat from the love they had made. She made it home and crawled into bed. She snuggled the pillow where Cade had just left, and she could still smell him. She fell asleep gazing at the beautiful ring that he had so sweetly put on her finger.

CHAPTER 5

Cade traveled back to his house with a heavy heart. He had to find a way that he could spend more time with her. He drove in his garage and grabbed his cell phone and went inside. He suddenly realized that if he could not be with her, maybe he could at least talk to her more. He would get her a cell phone! He would tell her what time he could call her, and they could talk for as long as it was possible. One thing is for certain, he had to find a way for them to be together soon. The sun was coming up when he decided to get a shower. He hated to wash his body that still smelled of his sweet Rebecca. He relived every moment of their lovemaking as he washed her from his body. He was drinking his coffee when his cell phone rang. It was the private investigator that he had hired the day before to find the woman for John. "Cade, this is Greg Peterson. I just wanted you to know that after I left you yesterday, Ms. Douglas went to a local bookstore and purchased some book on Amish religion. I am not sure how that is relevant, but you said you wanted to know every move this girl made till you tell me otherwise," explained Greg. "Thank you, Greg, keep me posted," stated Cade. He could not help but find this confirmation that the babies that this girl had were in fact John's.

Rebecca woke up after only a short time of sleeping, feeling refreshed as she drank her coffee, she wondered if Cade was thinking about her like she was him. She picked up her coffee cup and discovered that she had not taken her ring off. She quickly slipped it from her finger, giving it one last glance before putting it into a jar with trinkets that she kept in her cupboard. She sat down to eat a slice of pound cake when she heard a knock at her door. John made his way into the kitchen without Rebecca coming to open it. She was so glad to see him. "John, I am so glad you are here. I have something to show you," she said with haste in her voice. "Come with me to my room!" John followed her to her bedroom where she retrieved something from a shelf in her closet. When she showed the picture to John, his eyes filled with tears. Rebecca knew that he was as convinced as she was that the babies were in fact his. After giving him a moment to let the reality of it all sink in, she said, "John, you are a father to two little ones. From what I can tell, they are both dressed in blue, which means you have two little sons. You have got to find a way to talk to this woman." John put his head in his hands and said, "Rebecca, how am I going to do that!" "I'm not sure, John, but we will have to figure something out," Rebecca said as she paced the floor. "I am not sure when I will see Cade again, but I will see if there is any way for him to help." John looked at her with a look that told him he knew that they had slept together. "You saw him last night?" Rebecca shook her head yes. "John, I am convinced that he is trustworthy. I love him so much. He did not do anything out of the way. It was I that kissed him first. I could not help myself. I have something else to show you," she said with excitement in her voice. When they returned to the kitchen, she pulled the jar from the cupboard. She slid the ring back on her finger. John looked at the ring and said, "Rebecca, that is a two-carat blue diamond, do you have any idea what that would cost? I would not dare to say anything less than twenty-thousand dollars. Is this man rich?" "Yes, he said that he was. He also bought us a house yesterday with lots of land. He said that I can do with it anything that I want." John's head was reeling with all that he had learned. He was a father and Rebecca had given herself to an Englishman. He sat in the kitchen chair like he had been hit with a plow. He had to know the truth about the babies. He knew that he had made a commitment, but he would never be able to forgive himself if he was their father and did not at least try to win them back. "Look, we will figure out something. I promise! Mother sent me over here to tell you that the errand she asked you to do for her is tomorrow and if you were still going." he explained. "Yes, tell Mother that I am still planning to go. What time does she want me there?" she asked. John said nine in the morning. He got up and went home. Rebecca filled her day with baking and cleaning the house. She often cleaned when something was bothering her. It was getting dark before she realized that her outside chores were not done. She hurried to the barn to feed the livestock when she heard something coming up from the road. She could not tell who it was at first because of the light, and then she saw it was Ezekiel. "Hello, Rebecca, how are you this fine evening?" he said with a chipper tone. "I am well, Ezekiel, thank you for asking. What brings you out so late?" she asked. "Well, I am just returning from town and thought it would not hurt if I dropped by a moment. I brought you these!" Ezekiel said as he handed her a bouquet of flowers that he had gotten from town. "Thank you, they are beautiful!" she said, trying not to show her true emotions. "I just want you to know, Rebecca, I think of you often. I am quite busy at the moment, but there is hardly a day that goes by that I do not think of you. I must be on my way, Mary Grace is at her grandmother's, and I am to pick her up." He tipped his hat in courtesy and reined his buggy back toward the road. Rebecca was touched by the gesture; however, she was not attracted to him at all. She knew whom she wanted, and by God's grace, she hoped she could have him. She finished up with her chores and returned to the house. She put the lovely flowers in a vase of water and went upstairs to bath. She was considerably restless tonight, and Cade was on her mind so much that she could still taste his wonderful lips. She tossed on the bed for a while when she decided she would saddle Daniel's horse and go to the ball field to see if that would help her calm her restless soul. She got down and tied her horse and walked into the clearing. When she rounded the corner, she was startled at what she saw. *Cade!* She ran to be in his arms. He held her tightly and kissed her lips and face. "What are you doing here?" she said breathlessly. "I came here hoping that you missed me as much as I missed you and you would show up," he explained. Still shocked that he was there, she replied, "Oh, I am so glad you did! I have thought of nothing but you all day." "How long can you stay?" he asked. "I can stay as long as you want me to," she answered. "Well then, you will never go back then if that is the case!" Cade said as he squeezed her tighter. She had worn her nightdress and had put a shawl around her to keep the chill away. "Oh, Rebecca, you look so good," he said in a husky voice. "I am sorry I left in a hurry and was not thinking and it is chilly tonight," she responded. "I have a jacket in the car, would you like for me to get it for you?" he asked as he rubbed her arms to generate heat. "I am so stupid, would you like to sit in the car? Do you see what you do to me?" Rebecca laughed at the thought of her actually having that kind of effect on someone, and answered, "Yes, if that is okay." Cade opened the door to the backseat, and Rebecca got in. When she got in, her shawl fell, and he quickly grabbed it. He handed it to her as he got in. He caught a glimpse of her nightgown that gave no concealment to her body underneath. He sucked in and said, "Rebecca, baby, you are so beautiful you drive me wild," he said as he put her shawl back around her shoulders. Rebecca's heart melted because she knew he was genuinely glad to see her. He had no idea of just sleeping with her again tonight. "Rebecca, I want to ask you something. What do you think about the idea of having a cell phone? I could call you every night, and we could talk. I will show you how to use it, and if you cannot talk for some reason, then you can leave it off and I will understand," Cade explained. Rebecca thought about it for a moment and answered, "I think that is a great idea!" Cade reached in the glove box of his car and pulled a cell phone out. He explained, "I have already programmed my number in, so all you need to do is pull it up and push the green button." She was amazed that he had thought about getting her one and then actually went and got it. He had missed her no doubt. "Okay, that is simple enough. I can do that," she said with a smile. "I will call you at ten o'clock every night that we do not meet. If one of your brothers stay or something, just leave it off, and I will know that you could not talk. Oh yeah! Speaking of your brother. The private investigator that I hired to find Kelly Douglas called me this morning and told me he had followed her to a local bookstore. She bought books on the Amish religion." Rebecca's mind began to race. "The only reason someone would buy books on the Amish is if they were interested in learning about them, right?" she exclaimed. "Yes, baby, I guess you are right," Cade agreed. "Cade, would you be able to get her number by any chance?" she asked. "Yes, I can," he quickly answered. "If you can do that, maybe John can call her from this phone, and they can try to work this out," she said, shaking her head. "Yes, that is a great idea, honey!" he said, as though he were excited for him. Cade pulled her close to him and once again kissed those full red lips. When he pressed her up against him, he could feel her breast through her nightgown. "Oh my god, baby," he whispered in her ear. "I would love to make love to you right now. However, I am not going to take you in the backseat of my car," he said in a lust-filled voice. "Well then, let's go back to my house," Rebecca replied. Cade looked at her as if she were joking. It was Rebecca that started gathering up her things that he knew she in fact was serious. "Are you sure that is okay, Bec?" Cade asked. She kissed him passionately, watching his expression. He opened his eyes and saw her looking at him. He immediately started to get out of the car. He followed her to her horse and repeated what he had done the night before. They had safely made it inside her house. He held her close and kissed her sweet lips once more. Rebecca said, "I am going to get some water, I am very thirsty." Cade followed her with her lit candle to the kitchen. She went to the cupboard to grab a glass when he spotted the flowers sitting on the table. "The flowers are lovely, did you grow these?" he asked. "No, I did not, those were given to me by someone," Rebecca said as she filled her glass with water from the pitcher pump at the sink. She did not notice the look on Cade's face. She thirstily drank the water down and offered Cade something. He answered, "No, thank you. May I ask who gave these to you?" Rebecca could see his face clearly now as the lit candle had gotten closer. "They were given to me by Ezekiel King. He is a widower that has expressed interest in me," she said timidly. Cade went over to the sink and ran his hands through his long wavy black hair. Rebecca could see that he was blinded by jealousy. "Cade, you have nothing to worry about. He came by right after we met for the first time. He did ask me to marry him, but I have not given him an answer yet." As soon as she was finished, she realized how that sounded. She immediately began to explain. "It is not that way, Cade. He asked my father's permission to call on me, and it was given. I do not love him nor do I desire to be his wife. I am in love with you," she said as she went over and cupped her hand on his face. "Rebecca, I am not playing a game here. I love you, and I want you to be my wife. If I have not made my intentions clear, then maybe I need to try harder," he protested. "This is not a game to me either. I am deeply in love with you. I have even given myself to you out of wedlock. I have told you the truth," she said firmly. Cade held her close to him. He buried his face in her neck and began to kiss, softly whispering, "I will not lose you, Rebecca." He picked her up and carried her up the stairs as she held the small candle in her hand. When they had reached her room, he sat her down long enough to remove the nightgown from her. He gently laid her across the bed. He quickly removed his clothing and lay beside her as he caressed her beautiful body. He kissed her full lips that parted to welcome his tongue inside her. He kissed her neck until her body told of the desire she had for him. He captured her bosom with both hands and squeezed gently. The pink tips were erect and waiting for his attention. When he captured one of those tips in his mouth, Rebecca gasped for air. She could feel his hard member as it teased her inner thigh. She pulled him closer so she could reach it with her hand and slowly began to stroke it. Each stroke told her of his passion. He lifted himself from beside her and, with one hand, guided his throbbing manhood inside her. She let out a long hot breath. She looked him in the eyes as he began his thrusts inside her. He watched as her beautiful globes kept the rhythm of each one perfectly. He caressed her face lovingly yet passionately. As the rhythm got faster, her body danced violently. Cade could not stand the thought of another man wanting her. He brought his face down to hers, and as he nibbled on her lips, he said, "I love you, Rebecca, with a love that is true. I could not bear it if you chose another." Rebecca surrendered to his tongue and, as she grabbed the rock-hard buttocks that were delivering so much pleasure, whispered, "I only want you, my love, forever." Cade, with one quick motion, twisted her around so that she was on top of him. He guided his manhood back inside her and wrapped his hands around her tiny waist. He thrusts harder and harder inside her until he watched her body quiver uncontrollably. She gasped as the explosion left her breathless and quivering. Cade saw how violently her body had reacted, and he could not hold the flames of desire at bay any longer. She rode him as she drained every drop of seed from his body. He once again returned her to lay by his side and held her beside him until they were able to speak. Cade propped himself up on one arm so he could see her beautiful face and said, "I love you, Rebecca, with all my heart. I cannot bear this much longer." She ran her fingers through his black hair and replied, "I cannot bear being away from you much longer either. I am to go with my mother to see the doctor in the morning, let's hope that he has good news." Cade quickly interrupted, "I better go then and let you rest. I kept you up last night as well. I do not want you to become ill." He once again held her close to him as if he were soaking himself with her before he had to leave. They returned to his car, and he kissed her regretfully goodbye.

CHAPTER 6

Rebecca was fast asleep as the rooster started crowing. She dragged herself out of bed and dressed quickly. She had lots of chores to do before she was to meet her mother at nine. She made herself some coffee and carried it to the barn to care for her animals. She was startled from her daydreaming at the sound of someone approaching. "Oh!" she said, sucking in her breath and throwing her hay rake. Ezekiel stood there, and just as she was fixing to scold him for that, Mary Grace rounded the corner. "I am sorry, Rebecca, I seem to do that a lot. Is it me, or is your mind somewhere else these days?" Ezekiel said, almost admonishing her. "No, it is me, I have a lot on my mind these days, Ezekiel, and I do apologize. Good morning, Mary Grace, how are you this morning?" she said as she bent down on one knee and motioned for her to come sit on her lap. Ezekiel watched as she went over and gave Rebecca a hug. "We are headed into town this morning, and I was wondering if I might be able to get you something." Rebecca smiled and replied, "No, I am going myself in a bit. May I have a word with you, Ezekiel, alone?" He quickly told Mary Grace to go to the buggy and wait. Rebecca took a deep breath and began, "Ezekiel, you are a kind man. I am sure that you would make a wonderful husband, and I see that you are a wonderful father as well. However, I am not ready to marry, and I think that you are wasting your time here." Ezekiel hesitated for a moment and then asked, "How long do you think you might wait before you decide to take a husband? I will wait for you, Rebecca." He walked to her and pulled her out of sight of Mary Grace. She had no idea what he was about to do or she would have prevented it. Ezekiel took her into his arms and said, "I know Daniel was not a proper husband to you, Becca. I can be." He lowered his lips to hers and began to kiss her passionately. John walked in the barn and saw his sister pushing Ezekiel away. Although he was shocked by his behavior, he jerked him away, throwing him to the ground. Ezekiel was obviously embarrassed and said, "John, I meant her no disrespect, I merely wanted to show her that I could make her feel like a woman if she chose me," he said, pleading for understanding. The look on Rebecca's face told John all he needed to know. He was certain that he would have not pressed the issue any further with his daughter in the buggy, but nevertheless, he should have never made improper advances toward her at all. "Mr. King, I meant you no disrespect either, but I know Rebecca would have not allowed you to do that. I will never speak of this matter to anyone, but I must ask you to leave and never return again or I will speak to my father," John said firmly. Ezekiel got to his feet and dusted himself with his hat and replied, "That will not be necessary, John. I will respect your wishes." He returned to his buggy and drove away. John asked, "Are you all right?" "Yes, I am fine. Thank you for coming when you did. I had just told him that I did not want to marry him. I am afraid that I hurt him, and that was not my intention. It is just that he brought Mary Grace this morning. I did not want her to think that she was going to get a new mother. I have made my decision. I am just not certain of the timing. I am going with Mother to the doctor this morning, and we will see what he says. You were right, she is pregnant." John gave her an unpleasant look and said, "Well, that is why I am here. Mother wanted me to come pick you up so that I could just drop you off after you were through with your errand. I will finish up here while you freshen up." Rebecca had gone to change her clothes and returned to the porch where John was waiting for her. She climbed into the buggy and began to say, "John, I have a way for you to contact Kelly, but I will not have the number until tonight. Cade purchased me a cell phone so that he could call me on the nights we would not meet. You may use it to contact her. Cade is supposed to get the phone number today. He also said that the man he hired to find her saw her going into a bookstore. John, she purchased book about Amish religion." His face was pale with shock. "Why would she purchase books about us?" he asked. "Think, brother, why would you purchase books on a subject?" she said sarcastically. He immediately answered, "To learn more about it!" John's mind was racing; maybe she had had a change of heart when she realized the babies were his. He silently prayed to God that he would help him work this out.

Rebecca and her mother headed to town together and shared small talk on the way. It was when Mary brought Ezekiel up that Rebecca's countenance saddened. She knew she could not avoid the subject any longer. "Mother, I told Ezekiel this morning that I did not want to be his wife. I am not yet ready to remarry." Mary gave her a shocked look and, after being silent for a moment, asked, "Why, may I ask?" "Mother, I do not love him. I was married long enough to Daniel to know that I had rather lived alone and childless than to live with a man that I do not love. I know you said that you and Father were just friends when you married, but Daniel and I were more like brother and sister. I am sorry that he died, but I am not sorry to be out of that marriage. I know this is going to upset Father, but I cannot help the way I feel." Rebecca suddenly realized that she had went on and on about this matter. She quickly decided to say nothing else on the matter but said playfully, "Mother, I am sorry, the last thing you need right now is me unloading my problems on you. You have enough to contend without me opening more." Mary smiled at her daughter's attempt to change the subject and quickly replied, "Rebecca, your father and I did start as friends, however, later we fell in love, and I have never regretted marrying him for a moment. I can imagine that there are instances that two people that are not right for each other and, if they were to marry, could never be more than friends. You cannot let that keep you from getting married and being happy. Ezekiel is a fine man and look at the good you would be doing Mary Grace. Please reconsider your decision." "I will think on it, Mother, but I am pretty sure that I will not change my mind," Rebecca explained. They arrived at the doctor's, and much like on any other day, they had to endure the whispers and stares of the ever-watchful public eye. The English world for the most part was a friendly place, but on occasion, they do run upon someone that can be unkind. They walked in, and Mary had signed in. Rebecca was unusually nervous today. Her mind could not stop taunting her about the thought that she too could be expecting. She did not want to bring shame to her family; however, she did not regret her decision to give herself to a man that she loved very much. She was lost in thought when they called her mother's name. "Rebecca, are you coming?" Mary asked. She immediately got up and headed in her mother's direction. She watched as they took her mother's blood pressure and ordered her to give a urine sample. The nurse smiled and said, "Congratulations, Mrs. Fisher, you are pregnant!" Mary smiled sweetly at the nurse and waited to be put into an exam room. When the nurse showed her what room to go into, Rebecca followed behind her. Dr. Blevins catered to a lot of Amish women, and his office was set up for extra modesty. He had fixed all rooms with a curtain to pull around the patient in case their husband or family member wanted to join them for their visits. Rebecca seated herself in such an area and waited for her mother to undress. Dr. Blevins came in and, with a stern look on his face, said, "Mary, I cannot say that I am glad to see you in this condition, however, there is nothing we can do about that now." He examined her uterus and continued, "I want you to go to the ultrasound department, and I will talk to you after they are through." Mary did as the doctor told her to do. When she saw the picture of her already tiny baby, Mary could not help but cry. Rebecca watched the monitor as she saw her sibling come into view. She was amazed at what she saw. How precious life was, and if she were pregnant, she would be thrilled no matter the situation. Dr. Blevins returned to look at the findings. "Mary, I am pleased with what I see so far. We will just take it one day at a time. I do not want you to do any hard work or heavy lifting. I also want to see you back in two weeks. You are going to need to be watched closely." He patted her shoulder and continued, "Congratulations! You are due around the first of December." Dr. Blevins left, and Mary got dressed. They headed back toward home. The women were talking about the new arrival when Rebecca caught a glimpse of a familiar car. Cade could not help himself; he had followed her just to be able to look at her. Rebecca smiled at the thought of him missing her so bad when they had only parted hours ago. Rebecca reined the horse for home as the green light signaled. She could not wait to talk to him again.

Cade had been watching Rebecca and her mother for a while. He sat and daydreamed about bringing Rebecca to the obstetrician. He knew the possibility was already there. He had not turned at the light that led to Rebecca's house; he did not want to draw attention.

Rebecca had gotten back to her house and was exhausted. She had been up for two days now with little sleep. She lay down on the couch for a moment and unexpectedly drifted off to sleep. She woke up to a room that had already started to darken from the fading sun. She bolted up and began to rush to the barn. She finished her chores in record time and continued to the house to do the same. It was already Thursday, and she had not prepared a thing to go to the market. She pulled out her baking utensils and began to bake bread. She kept a watchful eye on the time. She knew that Cade would call soon. She had pulled the bread out of the oven when the phone rang. "Hello, my love," she answered. Cade almost melted when he heard that response. "Hello, my angel, how are you?" he replied. "I am well, I fell asleep on the couch and did not wake up till almost sunset," she said reluctantly. Cade laughed at the thought. "Baby, you were tired! It is my fault, I am the one to keep you awake." Rebecca could not wipe the grin from her face. "Well, I would not say that is your entire fault. It is not as though you twisted my arm." Cade loved the sound of her voice. It was doing strange things to his body. "What are you doing now, my love?" he asked. "I just got my bread out of the oven. I have six more loaves to bake, and I will be finished," she said. "Rebecca, I told you that you did not need to worry about the market. I will be more than happy to give you what you need," he said emphatically. "Thank you very much, you are so good to me, however, I do not need to draw attention to myself, and I am, after all, a widow. It is what is expected of me," she explained. "Bec, I cannot stand being away from you. I am sorry if you thought I was following you today. I just missed you so bad I needed to see you even if I could not touch you," Cade said with firmness. "I loved it!" Rebecca said with a giggle. "Dr. Blevins said that everything looked good so far. He told Mother that we would take it one day at a time," she said worriedly. "Cade, when I saw that tiny speck on the monitor, I started to cry. It was so precious and amazing!" Rebecca said so enthusiastically. Cade quickly said, "I can only imagine. I sat in the car and daydreamed about bringing you and finding out you were pregnant. I want so badly to have children with you. I know you are going to be a fantastic mother. I love you, baby." He finished sweetly. Rebecca wanted that too. She thought about John and the reality of his children. He hoped that he would one day soon be able to see them. "Bec, I have that number for John. I will text it to you," he said. "What is that?" Rebecca asked in total bewilderment. Cade laughed at her ignorance of modern technology. "Oh, my sweet baby! I have a lot to teach you, don't I? I will type the number in on my phone, and it will send it to yours. You will have a little note come up on your phone that says Message. It will have an option to read it on there, and it will show you what I have typed," he very patiently explained. "Oh my word, what will they think of next that is amazing!" Cade was thrilled to be the one to open her eyes to the world around her. They spent almost all night on the phone. The realization of what day of the week it was and that she had almost nothing to carry to market pulled Rebecca out of bed with the chickens. She worked all day gathering enough stuff to fill her buggy for the next day. She had just stopped for a cup of coffee when John came in the house. She was glad to see him; she wanted to tell him of her news. "Hello, brother, how are you today?" she asked, smiling. "I am scared to death if you must know. I am scared of her rejecting me yet again. I am scared that she may reject me even if the babies are mine. I am scared of having to explain this to Father and eventually the bishop," John said as he paced back and forth. "John, just settle down. The first step is to call her and see if she will talk to you. I have her number written down here. Take the phone and go into my room. I will watch out for someone who'll drive up," she urged. John took the phone and disappeared for hours. When he emerged, Rebecca could tell that he had been crying. "Well, it is obvious you have talked to her," she said, as if she wanted him to tell her more. "Yes, we have. The boys are mine, Rebecca. She was not sleeping with someone else. I was wrong. She said she could prove it by doing a paternity test if I wanted to." Rebecca put her hands over her mouth. She took a step backward as the reality set in. "Bec, she says she has missed me terribly. She wanted to tell me all of this, but she did not know how to contact me. She went to the market several times but never saw me, and she was not going to send word by anyone. Rebecca, I have got to see her. Please think of something that we can get away with for at least a day," John begged. She thought for a moment. "I will ask you to escort me to town under the pretence of shopping. I am getting low on a few things, and I will tell them that my list is long. How is that?" she asked. "I think that will work. When do you want to do this plan?" John anxiously asked. "I know you would love to do this as soon as possible. Tomorrow would not be good because Father will be at the market. We will do it early Monday!" she said nervously. John shook his head and left to call Kelly back and tell her of their plans. Rebecca sat on her porch and was trying to plan this out. She would get Cade tonight to help. John returned shortly and said, "It is set. I am to meet her Monday at her house. Her parents are away for a few days. We will have all day to hash this out," John said as he handed the phone back to her.

When Cade called her that night, Rebecca told him of their plans and asked him to help with the arrangements. Cade said, "I can pick the both of you up somewhere and bring him to her house and drop him off. The only thing I am not sure about is where to leave your buggy. I will have to leave it somewhere that it can stay for a while." Rebecca knew where she could leave it. There is a feed store where they leave their buggies at for a long time. "I can leave it at Miller's Feed in the back, there is a shaded lot that we use to leave buggies when we need to go into town for a long time. John and I will catch the bus and can be dropped off at the shopping plaza," Rebecca carefully explained. "Can you spend the day with me?" Cade asked. "Yes! I would love to, Cade," she very enthusiastically replied. "Okay then, I will make plans for us. I will let you get some sleep, and I will see you tomorrow, my love." They said their goodbyes that took several minutes. When Rebecca had gotten into bed, she was elated at the idea of being able to spend the day in Cade's world with him. She wondered what his home looked like and if they would make sweet love again. She fell asleep thinking of all the wonderful possibilities. She awoke with the excitement of being able to see Cade today. She loaded her buggy and set off to the market. She backed her buggy up to her tent as she usually did and noticed that John had Father's tent by himself again. She smiled at her brother and worked steady to unload and arrange her goods. She opened the curtain, with people already there. It was about an hour later that Cade arrived. He meandered much in his usual fashion. When he came to her tent, she wanted so badly to kiss him. She motioned for him to follow her, and they once again visited the privacy room in the back. Rebecca kissed him passionately. Cade grabbed her and very lustfully lifted her thigh to his waist as he held her tight buttocks in his hand. This lust-filled embrace only lasted seconds before returning to the front of the tent. Ezekiel had been unloading some furniture for Mrs. King when he had seen the Englishman going into the room with Rebecca. He walked to a place that would afford him a better view of what they were doing. The view was very limited, but he watched as Rebecca threw herself passionately into his arms. The sting of rejection was still fresh on his mind. He now knew why she did not want him as her husband. She had reduced herself to being an Englishman's whore. Ezekiel was furious. He could not stand the thought of him touching her. He also could not stand the thought of her liking it either. He came to the realization that if he said anything about it, John would go to the bishop and tell him how he had acted that day in her barn. It would be their word against his. He was deeply troubled as what to do. He would take Rebecca even if she were forced by her father to marry him. He loved her and thought she was the most beautiful woman he had ever seen. He had lain in his bed many nights thinking of how she had looked with her hair down. His body ached to have her. He had asked for forgiveness several times. However, he had not been able to control this feeling he had for her. When he had seen her that day with her hair down, he had envisioned her naked before him. His body ached to touch her, to make love to her. He wanted desperately to have her in his bed. Cade had left, being careful no to linger too long. He had briefly talked with John and said his goodbye. By afternoon, almost all of the people had vanished, and John decided to leave early. Rebecca wanted to stay a bit longer and told him to go ahead. She had gone to her privacy room to start packing her things when Ezekiel stepped in. "Rebecca, I wish to speak to you. I behaved badly the other day, and I want to again say that I am truly sorry for my actions," Ezekiel said, trying to keep the sting of rejection from his face. "I want to make amends, if I may, by giving you this settee for your porch," he said as he fidgeted with his hat. "May I drop it off on my way home? I will be leaving shortly." Rebecca thought a moment and said, "Yes, that will be fine, Ezekiel, although that is really not necessary. Your apology was enough." "No, I feel I must do this for you," Ezekiel urged. Rebecca continued, "I will be leaving shortly myself. I am tired, and I will be turning in early tonight." They loaded up, and Ezekiel followed behind her as she made her way home. When they arrived, Rebecca pulled up to the porch and offered her assistance in unloading the beautiful wooden furniture that he had made. She showed him where to set it and thanked him kindly. "Would you like a glass of lemonade or a cup of coffee perhaps before you leave?" she said, hoping he would have the decency to turn it down. "A cup of coffee would be wonderful, thank you, Rebecca," he answered. He sat at the new furniture, setting his hat on the table to imply he would wait there. Rebecca went into the kitchen and began preparing the coffee. She was getting cups from the cupboard when Ezekiel came up behind her. He grabbed her under her arms and squeezed her full chests. He said in a husky voice, "I am a good lover, Becca. I will not leave you wanting for a thing. It is a shame to let those beautiful tits go unattended." He pulled her to him and began kissing her neck. She could feel his swollen manhood on her buttocks that was threatening to burst through his trousers at any moment. He squeezed one of her round globes while he rubbed her womanly place firmly. Rebecca was shocked at his behavior. She was panic-stricken, and her first thought was Cade. He would be so angry. She felt as if she were cheating on him. She tried to move away from the grip he had on her; however, he was a very strong man, and her attempts were futile. "Ezekiel, please don't do this, think about Mary Grace and what this would do to her if she knew," she pleaded. Ezekiel replied as he jerked her around to face him. "What Mary Grace needs is a brother or sister to play with, and I want you to be the one to give it to her." He pulled at her pinafore, and it fell to the floor. He did not take time to remove the pin from her blouse and ripped it open as well. The pin that held it together came down and cut her in its descent to the floor. Rebecca stood there even more dazed than before. She watched as Ezekiel looked at her naked skin. He pushed himself against her harshly and was squeezing her against the counter. He kissed her naked chest wildly as he pulled at her corset to loosen it. When her breasts were free, she knew that he was going to rape her. She began to beat his back with her fists. He pushed her to the ground and had pulled her skirt up when she saw the rolling pin on the shelf nearby. She pretended not to fight anymore so he would let his grip on her loosen. He sat up enough that he could pull his throbbing member from his pants. As he knelt there, with it in his hand, he said, "You will not tell anyone about this, you whore! I saw you today with the Englishman. You were not fighting him off. How long has he been bedding you, Rebecca? Are you bred yet? Well, you better hope so because if you are not, I am fixing to breed you myself!" Ezekiel was about to enter her when the blow came. She hit him straight across the temple. When he fell, she got up and pulled her clothes together. The thought of what he had just said still rang in her ears. Ezekiel knew about Cade! It would only be a matter of time before everyone knew about it. She paced the floor in front of him and suddenly realized. He would not tell a soul. She would show the clothes and the scratch to John, he would be her witness to the attack. She would tell everyone of the attempted rape and have the evidence to prove it! She grabbed her torn clothes and clutched them to cover her naked chest. Ezekiel came to with Rebecca standing over him. She was crying pitifully, and she was holding the rolling pin in her hand. Ezekiel shook his head to clear the fog that he had been left with. As he stood to his feet, he grabbed the counter to steady his feet, when his head stopped spinning, he reached for his trousers that had pooled around his ankles. "Get out, Ezekiel, and do not ever return here. I will tell everyone what you had done here today!" she shouted. Ezekiel put his head in his hands. He replayed in his mind what had just happened. "Rebecca, please forgive me. Can't you see how much I care for you? How much I need you. I go to bed at night thinking of you beside me. Please forgive me. When I saw you kissing that man today, I felt as though you had stuck a knife to my heart. Please know that I would do anything to have you, Rebecca," he said, pleading with tears running down his face. "I do not love you, Ezekiel. I am in love with the Englishman, and I am going to be with him. I will never speak of this to no one, but if you say anything about the Englishman, I will go straight to my father and I will go to the bishop. I will take the evidence with me. I am also going to show John this." She released her shirt just enough to let Ezekiel see the cut that his brutality had left. She was crying uncontrollably, clenching the rolling pin in her hand. Ezekiel knew the damage that he had done could never be reversed. He once again said, "Rebecca, I am truly sorry," as he left. Rebecca listened as he drove away. She squatted back on her heels and sobbed uncontrollably. When the pain of what had just happened subsided a little, she brought her buggy to the barn. The sun set, and Rebecca sat on a pile of hay and cried pitifully. She needed Cade; she wanted his arms around her. She needed him desperately; she wondered what time it was and ran to the house. The grandfather clock struck eight o'clock just as she came in the house. She ran upstairs to get her phone. She needed him, and she could not wait another two hours. Through tear-filled eyes she tried to find out how to pull his number up on the screen. After several failed attempts, she finally heard the phone ring. "Rebecca?" Cade said with a worried tone. "Is everything okay, baby?" he continued. "Cade, I need you, can you please meet me at the ball field?" Rebecca said, crying. Cade could hear the panic in her voice. "Yes, I can, I am leaving right now!" She threw the phone on her bed and quickly changed. She arrived at the meeting place to find Cade had just pulled up. He ran to her when he saw her. Cade saw that she was still crying and asked, "What is the matter, baby? Do we need to leave now?" Rebecca's mind was reeling. She wanted to, but the thought of her mother quickly came to her mind. Cade, quickly seeing that she was obviously very upset about something, pulled her to him and held her tight. He kissed her lips until she seemed to be calmer. He kissed her neck and was shocked as she yelped in pain. "What is the matter, Rebecca, are you hurt? Please tell me," he pleaded as he lifted her shirt to see. When he saw the gash that was still bleeding a little, he asked with a firm tone, "Who did this to you?" Rebecca put her hand over her mouth. She did not want to tell him, she was scared he would be mad with her. Her thoughts were interpreted. "Bec, please tell me what happened. You can tell me anything, baby. I want you to tell me everything," Cade pleaded. Rebecca took a deep breath to calm herself and began. "Cade, the other day, Ezekiel dropped by to see if I needed anything from town. I told him that I was not going to marry him. He grabbed me and kissed me. He said that he was a good lover and that he would not leave me wanting. John walked in and caught him kissing me. He jerked him off me and threw him to the ground. Ezekiel was furious. John told him not to return to my house or he would tell Father. Today at the market, he saw you and me kissing. I had no idea though. When I was loading my things up this afternoon, he approached me and told me how sorry he was for what had happened. He went on to say that he wanted to give me some furniture for my porch as a token of how sorry he was. I told him that was not necessary, that his apology was enough. He insisted on giving the furniture. When I agreed, he came to drop it off. I thanked him and offered something to drink. Cade, when I went to the kitchen to fix it, he came in there with me." Rebecca cried uncontrollably. Cade could tell by her reaction what had happened. He held her tight as she cried. He was consumed with jealousy; this stupid man had taken this beautiful, innocent woman—*his* woman. The thought of him touching her made his blood boil. He wanted to hit something so bad. He took in a long breath and tried to control his anger. "Are you okay? I mean, he did not hurt you physically?" Cade asked with persistence. "No other than the cut. It happened when he ripped my blouse off," she said as she cried. Cade lost it. The image of that man ripping her shirt off sent a knife through his heart. "Rebecca, I want you to get in the car with me right now! I want you to take me to this man's house. When I am finished with him, he will regret the day that he ever set foot on your property." He released her and ran both hands through his black hair. He turned and went back to Rebecca and said, "I need to carry you to the emergency room, Bec, they can take semen samples. You could put him in jail for a long time. Is there anything at your house that you want to take with you because I am not bringing you back here ever. Rebecca realized at that point that Cade thought he had been successful in his attempt to rape her. "Cade, he did not take me. I hit him with my rolling pin, and he fell to the floor," she said, calming some. He was so relieved he immediately grabbed her and kissed her forehead. "Thank God," he whispered. "I told him that I love you, and I was going to be with you, and if he told anyone about us, I would tell everyone that he raped me. I kept my clothes, and I am going to show John my cut," she explained. "Oh, Bec, you did so well! I am so proud of you, baby," Cade said as he gently squeezed her. "If you would like, I will come lie beside you while you sleep tonight," he suggested. "I would love that, my angel," Rebecca said as she finally smiled. When they had made it to her house, she held Cade's hand until they were in the bedroom. He removed his shirt and shoes and crawled into bed. Rebecca was unsure how to remove her clothes if they were not going to make love. She was in a quandary when she decided to turn her back to him. He watched as she removed her blouse and skirt. It was when she lifted her slip that his body began to beg for her. He saw a hint of her full breast as the slip released its hold on them. He could see the beautiful curve of her hips and the smooth creamy skin as the flames of the candle flickered, and he yearned to touch it. He knew that she did not want nor need this tonight. She needed him to be gentle and sincere, and as long as he was near her, that was all that mattered to him. When she turned to come to bed, he gasped at the full view of her. She was so perfect. He thought he was the luckiest man on earth. Rebecca settled in next to him, her warm skin against his sent his body into fits. He was fighting to keep his body from showing signs of him wanting her. It was when she pressed her full bosom up against his chest that he had to bite his lip. Rebecca could feel his heart beating madly. She wondered what was causing it when she looked up at his face. He had his eyes closed and was biting his lip. "Cade, what is the matter?" she asked innocently. Cade was not sure if he should explain or just change the subject. "Rebecca, I am sorry, it is just being near you like this and feeling you next to me, well, to be honest, I am having a hard time controlling myself, but that is okay, you have been through too much today. I really did want to let you sleep in my arms." Rebecca rose up to his lips and kissed him passionately and, with a heated, passion-filled voice, said, "Cade, make love to me. Show me again what it is like to be loved by a man that loves me." The look on her face and to hear those words were all Cade could take. He moved her tenderly under him. He kissed her gently all over. He caressed every inch of her body. He could hear her as she took long hard breaths as he made sweet love to her. He wanted to remove all thoughts of Ezekiel and how he had tried to take her. He wanted her to feel loved and protected, and above all else, he wanted her to feel loved.

CHAPTER 7

Rebecca had decided not to attend the church meeting today. She could not bear the thought of seeing Ezekiel. This week's meeting was going to be held at his mother's home. She knew her parents would worry, but she would say she was ill. After all, that was not a lie. She was ill. She was still upset over the ordeal. Cade had been so sweet last night. She was still amazed at the effect he had on her. He only had to look at her, and she melted. She loved him dearly and was very thankful that she had found someone that really understood her. She could hardly wait till Monday. She was going to be with him all day. Because the Amish do no work on Sunday, Rebecca lay around all day. She thought of Cade and how she missed him. It was almost dark when she heard a buggy coming up the drive. She went to the door and saw that it was John. Her father had probably sent him to check on her after she was not at church today. Rebecca stood in the doorway as he got down from the buggy and came in. She closed the door behind him. He asked, "Everything okay? Why were you not at church today?" Rebecca looked down at her feet and began to cry. John's first thoughts were Cade had left her. Rebecca said through the tears, "I want to show you something." She opened the collar of her blouse so that John could see the cut Ezekiel left on her neck. "Rebecca, I swear I will hurt him!" John said as he got up and started to stomp out of the door. "John, it was not Cade! Yesterday as I was leaving the market, Ezekiel came to me and again apologized for what happened. He said he wanted to give me a settee as a gesture for his behavior. I told him that was not necessary. When he insisted, I agreed. When he dropped it off, I offered him something to drink to be polite. I was in the kitchen, and he came up to me. He almost raped me!" She dried her tears as John came to her and knelt beside her. "Rebecca, did he—?" "No, thank God, I hit him with a rolling pin that I managed to get from the shelf. He had me pinned to the floor, and he ripped my blouse off me. The pin came undone, and it made the cut. I could not bear to face him this morning." John got up and walked out the front door. Rebecca was afraid that he was headed to Ezekiel's house. "John! Please do not go to his house. He saw me kissing Cade at the market. He knew why I do not wish to marry him." John turned around for a moment and then continued on to the barn. He came from the barn with an axe. He walked to her front porch where the new settee sat and began cropping it with the axe. Rebecca did not try to stop him; all she could do was cry. When John had made firewood out of the beautiful settee, he dropped in a nearby chair. Rebecca went over and sat next to him. "I told him that I was going to show you this cut and my clothes that he ripped. I also told him that if he said anything about Cade and me, we would go to Father and the bishop and tell them that he raped me." John shook his head in agreement and said, "I am still going to have a word with Mr. King!" he said with an anger-filled voice. "Please let it go, John. I will not have him to worry with anymore," Rebecca said. "Well, he was at church today. I wondered why he acted so strange. He was very quiet and kept to himself," John said with sarcasm. "When he left yesterday afternoon and I could already speak, I called Cade. He was beside himself. I think he would have gone after him if I had not stopped him." "I just hope that he believes I will do that if he says anything. I think he knows you will. You have nothing to lose and everything to gain. If you are sure that you are going to be all right, I am going to leave now. I will pick you up in the morning at eight."

Rebecca decided that she would spend the afternoon baking. She loved doing it, and she especially loved the smell of fresh baked bread drifting through the house. It always seemed to lift her spirits. Rebecca had just pulled her last loaf of sweet bread from her oven when she realized the time. She washed her hands and ran upstairs to get the cell phone Cade had bought for her. She lay in her bed and waited for the call. When the phone rang, Rebecca answered it speedily; she had missed Cade terribly. "Hello, my angel," she answered. The sound of her voice nearly took Cade's breath. "Hello, baby," Cade answered in a saddened whispered voice. "Cade, what is the matter, baby? Is there something wrong?" she asked urgently. Cade took a deep breath and began, "Rebecca, I cannot stand being apart from you, this is killing me. I have spent the day making plans for our future, and the reality is I don't know when that will start. I know you do not want to cause harm to your mother, neither do I, but, baby, I can't stand being away from you. I have thought about you all day, wondering if you are all right. I was also wondering if that bastard was trying to put his hands on you again. I love you, Rebecca, and if you want, I will go with you to tell your parents. I will suffer whatever the consequences may be." Rebecca could hear the desperation in his voice. She too had missed him terribly all day. She wanted nothing more than leave this place and be with him for the rest of her life. After a brief silence, Rebecca said, "Cade, let me see John through this tomorrow, and I will start making plans to leave. I need a week or two to decide what of this, if anything, I am going to bring. Is that all right?" Cade felt as though a weight had been lifted from his shoulders. He wanted so badly to hold her right at this moment. "I don't mean to beg, baby, I also don't want to put that kind of pressure on you. You mean the world to me, and I want so badly to be with you," he said softly. "I understand, my love. I want it as bad as you. I just do not want to make it worse for my mother. However, I cannot make my decision on the welfare of others. If I wait till the time is right, then I would be waiting forever because it is never going to be right." Cade was glad she had come to realize that. "I can't wait till tomorrow. I want to bring you to see the house. I am so excited for you to see it! I can't believe we get to spend the whole day together," Cade said with a little more cheer. He once again went over the arrangements and the time they would meet. Rebecca knew that she was going to have to shop quickly in the morning if she were to meet Cade at nine. She had to purchase her things in order for their shopping trip to look legitimate. She hated lying, and if it were possible to do it without lying, that is the way she wanted it. If they returned home tomorrow night with packages, she knew there would be no questions asked. "I am going to bed now. I want to be rested for my big day tomorrow. I am going to get up and be there at seven to get my shopping done. I also have to do my chores before I go," Rebecca stated. "I will be glad when you do not have to work so hard, my love. I want to spoil you every moment," Cade said sweetly. Rebecca went to sleep quickly; she was unusually tired these days. She knew it was because of the late hours that she had been keeping. When she woke up the next morning, she could not help but smile. She dressed in record time. She also finished her chores and was on her third cup of coffee when John arrived. She noticed his countenance and reassured him that everything was going to be fine. She hopped in the buggy, and they drove away. When they arrived at the General Store, Rebecca made her choices. She paid for the items and asked the cashier to load her items in the buggy and notified him that she would be gone for a while. She and John caught the bus across town and arrived at their meeting spot a few minutes early. A huge smile began to build on Rebecca's face when she saw that Cade was already there.

He got out and opened the door for Rebecca as she got into the car. John sat in the backseat. Cade held her face in his hands and gave her a loving quick kiss and said, "Hello, baby, I am so glad to see you! Hello, John, it's nice to see you again. I am sure that your stomach is filled with butterflies. I must say I am glad it is you and not me. I must tell you that Rebecca and I will do whatever you need us to today. I will be out-of-pocket for a little while first thing. I am bringing her out to see the house that I bought for us. Here is my cell phone number if you need to call us. While we are at the house, we are still no more than forty-five minutes away." John and Rebecca both were touched at his kindness. Rebecca, suddenly realizing that she had forgotten something, said, "I almost forgot! I brought this for you to take with you." She handed him the cell phone that Cade had gotten her. "I love you, John, and I pray that everything will work out for you." Cade drove up to Kelly's house and waited for her to answer the door before leaving. Rebecca was relieved some when Kelly had come to the door smiling. As they drove away, Cade grabbed her hand and kissed it and said, "He will be fine, baby, he knows what he is doing." Rebecca gave him a smile and rubbed her hand across his chiseled cheek. He was so beautiful. She could hardly believe that he was hers. "I have a surprise for you, my love. It will require me going to my apartment however. Is that all right?" Rebecca said, "Yes, of course!" When Cade turned into the drive, Rebecca could hardly contain herself. The apartment complex was beautiful. It was a gated community where only the uppermost class could afford. Cade pulled his car in his garage and closed the door behind them. He came around and opened the door for her, and when she had stepped out of the car, he pulled her to him, pinning her slightly against his car. He held her face in his hands and kissed her tenderly. "Rebecca, I am so glad you are here. I have wanted this for so long!" he said as he squeezed her tighter. Rebecca could not believe her eyes when he opened the door. It was like nothing she had ever seen before. It was definitely masculine but very beautiful. The kitchen was huge, and the stainless steel appliances were amazing. "Baby, would you care for something to drink? I have anything you would want. Would you care for a soda or tea?" he asked. "Actually, water would be great!" He went to the enormous refrigerator and pulled out bottled water and handed it to her. All this was so different from the way she lived. It overwhelmed her completely, and she wondered if she even belonged there for a moment. Cade watched her face as she looked around at everything in great detail. He could see that she was a bit overwhelmed. "Rebecca, I know all this may seem overwhelming to you, but we are just going to take this slow, and I am with you every step of the way. I thought my surprise might help and also might keep you from being recognized." Cade grabbed her hand and led her down the hall, when they had reached his bedroom, Rebecca was again amazed at the beauty of it. The huge four-poster bed that sat sideways in the room with suede coverlets and a TV that folded into the ceiling. The richness of the dark mahogany wood, leather, and suede curtains that hung from two ceiling-to-floor windows on the far wall of the room left her speechless. She could picture Cade sleeping there at night. Cade went and opened a door that led to a room filled with clothes. It had a settee with shopping bags of all kinds in there. "I went shopping yesterday. You were on my mind so strongly that I decided to surprise you with a start on your new wardrobe," Cade said as he pointed. Rebecca almost fainted; she could not believe that he had been that thoughtful. "I had to guess at your size, but I think I hit the nail on the head. I am going to sit here in my chair while you make your selection and change," he said, smiling at her amazement. He watched as she slowly went into the closet and chuckled out loud as she closed the door behind her. Her timidness still amazed him, and he thought it to be such a turn-on. Rebecca began to open the bags to see what was inside. She started with the smallest bag first. She reached inside and pulled out a bra and panty set. It was white with pink satin ribbons; it was beautiful to her. She could not wait to try it on. The corset bras that they wore were terribly uncomfortable and ugly. She looked in the mirror and frowned at the image of herself. She quickly began to remove her clothes, and she felt as if she were a caterpillar that was turning into a beautiful butterfly. She had put the set on and turned to look in the mirror. She gasped at the sight of her. She could not believe how she looked. Cade had guessed her size perfectly. The bra fit her perfectly and made her bosom stand to attention. The matching panties were very small and did not come the waist as her normal ones did. She took her hair down that had been French braided since last night, and it fell in wavy fullness around her. She was so happy that she had shaved her legs, and even though she had no makeup on like the Englishwomen wore, she felt so beautiful. She began pulling the other things from the bags. She was delighted when she saw that he had bought her a pair of the denim pants that almost every Englishwoman wore. Even Cade was wearing them today. When Rebecca slid them over her thighs, she was thrilled that they fit her like a glove. She turned to see what she looked like from behind and thought she looked sexy. When she had gone through the other bags, she had ran across a blue satin blouse that buttoned up the front with beautiful rhinestone buttons and a lovely sash that tied at the waist. She decided that this was the one she would wear. As she put the blouse on, she relished the buttons on the front. Amish clothes were not to have buttons. She always thought that to be so ridiculous because of the simplicity of their usefulness. She loved how her eyes matched her blouse and thought Cade would love it as well. She left her top button undone to give a hint of her full breast below. Rebecca saw a whole row of boxes on the floor and began to open them one by one, admiring the shoes that he had purchased. It was when she came to a pair of silver rhinestone sandals that she was positive which she wanted to wear. She placed them on her feet and looked at herself in the mirror. The rhinestones in the shoes reminded her of her engagement ring she had concealed in the toe of her shoe. She quickly retrieved it and slid it on her finger. Her eyes filled with tears as she saw the transformation. It took her several minutes to gain the courage to open the door. Although she felt more beautiful than she had ever felt, she was afraid that she might not measure up to the other Englishwomen she had seen. When she finally opened the door, Cade's face wiped away any doubt she could possibly have had. Cade could not believe how amazing she looked. The uniform of the Amish, as unattractive as they made them to be, still was made to be beautiful with her wearing them. Looking at her now simply took his breath away. When he was able to speak, he asked her to turn around. His body tingled at the sight of her perfect buttocks and how magnificent she looked. "Rebecca, I am the luckiest man alive. I can't tell you how amazing you look. I will be the envy of every man we meet today!" Rebecca smiled at his sweet words. He kissed her longingly and said, "One more thing before we leave." Cade went over to the tall highboy dresser that faced his bed. He pulled a small box from it and handed it to her. Rebecca opened it with trembling fingers, and when its contents came into view, she gasped, putting her hand over her mouth. Rebecca could not speak from the beauty of it. Cade asked, "Do you like it?" Rebecca felt as though she were in a fairy tale. She looked up at him with tears in her eyes and said, "If I am asleep, please do not wake me!" She held her hair up as he placed the beautiful blue diamond necklace on her that matched her engagement ring. She let her hair down and marveled in its beauty. She once again went to the box and adorned the earrings that completed the set. She was stunned at the wonderful surprises that he had given her. She turned to him and kissed him with a kiss that conveyed her every emotion. "Bec, I want every day of the rest of your life to be just like this. I want to show you the world and see it through your eyes. You amaze me at the way you see things. I love your innocence, please do not be embarrassed by it. I will make every day special for you, my love." He held her to him, breathing in her aroma. He knew that today would solidify their commitment to one another. Cade pushed her back to take one more look at her. She blushed when he made a face that suggested she was hot! He grabbed her hand and led her out to the kitchen. "Are you ready, soon-to-be Mrs. Matthews?" Rebecca loved the sound of that and shook her head yes. When they arrived at this beautiful restaurant, Cade opened the door, and a valet watched as he helped her get out. The valet said, "Good day, Mr. Matthews." Cade watched as the mouth of the valet, whom he had known for years, dropped at the sight of Rebecca. "May I say that I have never seen such a beautiful woman as she?" Cade smiled and said, "This is Rebecca Lapp, Vince. She is my fiancée." "Then may I say that you are one lucky man, Mr. Matthews," replied the valet. Rebecca blushed at the comment and said, "Thank you, that is very kind of you to say." Cade took her by the hand and entered the restaurant. He watched as everyone stopped and stared at Rebecca. When the host brought them to a table where a woman was sitting, Rebecca thought there had been some kind of mistake. "Rebecca, I hope that you will not be upset with me. I wanted you to meet my mother, and fearing that everything may overwhelm you, I decided to keep it a secret until we arrived." She smiled at the older woman and, extending a hand, said, "I am very pleased to meet you, Mrs. Matthews." "Please call me Gloria, Rebecca, and it is I who is pleased to meet you!" Gloria said as she shook her hand. Rebecca turned toward Cade and said, "I am not upset with you at all. I am actually grateful that I did not know. I had no time to fret over it." Gloria laughed at her honesty. Gloria could not help but notice how much in love they were. "I wanted to tell you that the pillowcases that you made were quite lovely. I have always admired the workmanship of the Amish. They are masters at their craft," Gloria stated. "Thank you very much. I do enjoy it. Although I suspect that my life is going to get far busier. I hope to find time to continue with it however," Rebecca replied. Cade sat back and was amazed at the ease in which Rebecca was talking with his mother. He suspected that she would be quite comfortable with meeting anyone. They shared their lunch together, and Cade was in awe at Rebecca's knowledge of many subjects. He knew not or even imagined her to be a stupid person. He merely thought that her sheltered life would not allow her to be knowledgeable on things of the outside world. He also knew that he did not have to ask for his mother's approval. It was quite obvious that she loved her! They had finished their meal and was about to leave the restaurant. Gloria said as she stood up, "Rebecca, it has been a pleasure meeting you, and I am so looking forward to visiting with you again. I hope it is not too long before we are planning a wedding. I want you to know that if things do not work out the way that you hope they will, I will be more than happy to help with the arrangements." Rebecca was shocked, it sounded as though she knew of her circumstances. Cade kissed his mother's forehead, and she walked out. Cade motioned to the waiter that he wanted the check. Rebecca asked, "Cade, does your mother know what I am?" Cade put his hand on her face and said, "Yes, she does! And it is not as though you are some kind of freak, baby. You are a beautiful, fantastic, precious, woman who just so happened to be raised Amish. You're not from Mars! I tell Mother everything. She knows everything about you that is proper for her to know." When the waiter arrived and Cade had paid for lunch, they walked out with Cade's arm around her waist. When they had reached the door, someone hollered, "Cade!" He looked in the direction it was coming from and said, "Alan! How are you, old buddy?" Alan held out his hand and then hugged him. "I am great but not as good as you, man. Who is this beautiful woman?" Cade smiled at Rebecca and said, "Alan, this is the love of my life and the woman that is soon going to be my wife! Alan, meet Rebecca Lapp." Rebecca held out her hand to shake his hand when he said, "I do not want a handshake from the woman that finally snagged this guy. I want a hug!" Alan hugged her and looked at Cade with a look of approval. "So when is the big day?" Alan asked. Cade answered, "Well, we are not really sure although it is going to be soon. We just bought a house in Great Mills. We bought the old Masterson Estate." Alan shook his head and said, "Yes, I know where that is. Are you from here, Rebecca? I know I have not seen you around." Rebecca said, "Yes, I am from here. Just outside of Mechanicsville." Alan said, "Well, I am so happy for you, Cade. It has been a long time coming. Let me know when it is, I will be there." Cade said, "Yes, I will. We are not sure if we are going to have big wedding but stay close, I may need a best man!" Alan laughed and said, "I would not miss this beautiful thing coming down the aisle for nothing." Rebecca's face turned red with the complement and said, "Thank you. You are too kind." Cade said, "Alan, it was good seeing you again, I am glad you are in town, and I will be in touch. We are on a tight schedule today, and we need to run." Alan watched as they were leaving and could not believe how sweet and innocent Rebecca was. He could not remember when he had last seen a woman blush. When he had gotten Rebecca in the car and as they drove away, he explained, "Alan and I were classmates for many years. We went to a private school together. He and I have kept in touch. We talk every six months or so. He is the best! His wife is awesome, and they have two children. Maggie is four, and Max is two by now. I used to love hanging out with them. But after the kids came, I always felt like the third wheel. Maybe it will not be too long before we have a little one to share with them." Rebecca squeezed his hand and said, "I will love it, and I love you so much, and this day had been so wonderful, and your mother is so nice! Oh, Cade, I feel like I am in a fairy tale. I do not want to go home tonight!" Cade listened to her and saw her excitement. He wanted this day to be the best day of her life, and he was sure that so far it had been. They shared ideas about a wedding as they drove to their soon-to-be home. When Cade turned off the main road, he said, "Our land starts here at the white picket fence and goes everywhere that you see." Rebecca loved it. It had that farmhouse look and feel. She felt as though she was at home already. When they pulled up to the house, she was astounded at the size of the house. It was three stories with tall pillars in front. The front porch was enormous and had tall oak trees on both sides of the yard. There was a three-carport garage at the end of a short cemented driveway that she was sure was added later. Cade walked over and opened the door for her and took her by the hand and led her as they walked up several stairs. He unlocked the door and led her inside. The foyer was amazing, and above it was a spiral staircase. It led to a huge living room. There was a balcony that overlooked the living room from above. Rebecca could not help but think of a bride as she made her way up the steps. "Cade, what do you think of having a wedding here? It is beautiful, and what better way than to celebrate our new house but for us to marry here," she said as she still was looking around. "Why haven't I thought of that? It is perfect!" Cade said as he rushed over to hug her. "This week when I come over, I will bring some catalogs, and we can start buying our furniture. I will have the whole house done and ready for our wedding and our life together," Cade said as he was bursting with joy. Cade kissed her tenderly. He loved her completely. When they were finished sharing ideas about the house, Cade knew their wonderful day was about to end. It was already midafternoon, and Rebecca still had to transform back into her cocoon. The ride back to the apartment was not as jovial as the rest of the day because they knew they would be parting soon. Cade drove into his garage and opened the door for Rebecca. She looked into his eyes as he pulled her to him and said, "Cade, I will tell my parents this week of my decision. I cannot stand the idea of going back tonight. Mother has a doctor's appointment Tuesday, and if all is well, I will tell them when we return." Cade returned to her lips with a passionate kiss that let her know that he needed her. He lifted her off her feet and carried her to his room. He sat her down gently and kissed her neck, kissing a trail that led to her full breast. He slowly undid the buttons on her shirt with one hand while he held her close with the other. As the last button was unfastened, he pushed open the satiny blouse, when he saw the white bra with the pink satin bows, he marveled in her beauty. He removed the blouse, and it fell to the floor. Rebecca undid her jeans and slid them over her hips seductively. Cade ran a hand through his black hair carefully as to not miss a minute of her beautiful body. Cade took off his shirt and basked in her beauty as she stood before him. She unhooked the bra, and the two perfect mounds bounced in delight. She gently removed the panties, sliding them over her pretty rounded hips until they were on the floor under her feet. Cade started to remove his jeans, and when he had unbuttoned them and began to slide them off, his huge throbbing member sprang into freedom. Rebecca boldly grabbed it and began to caress every inch of it. She watched as Cade delighted in it. His breathing was heavy, and his swollen member was about to explode. Cade lifted her off her feet and carried her to his bed. He looked longingly into two crystal pools that steamed with passion. He caressed her beautiful face that was flushed with pleasure. He rubbed her luscious body that lay beneath him. Cade reclaimed her full ruby red lips that were parted in anticipation of what was to come. Cade began to stroke the wet dark womanly spot that drove her wild. Her body began to move wildly as the pleasure was too much for her. Cade slid the throbbing member into her with firmness. She moaned loudly because of the pleasure that it brought. Cade slowed the rhythm so he could delight her further. Rebecca whimpered as the waves of passion were overtaking her. She clung to Cade as if she were taking her last breath. Cade continued to plunge his manhood into her until he himself found relief. His body quivered at the force of it. He continued to hold her in this position, enjoying the moment that they both were satisfied. He gently put his nose to hers and looked lovingly into her eyes. "Rebecca, I love you so much. I cannot wait till you are here. I want you to know you are my breath, my love. I need you with me," Cade said with such sweetness. Rebecca lay back on her pillow and traced the black mat that covered his chest. "I feel the exact same way. I do not want to leave today. I also need you. I have also given some thought to our lovemaking. I could never deny you, but I must tell you that the thought of me being pregnant does concern me. I want to have your children, but I do not want to bring shame on my family. I know that I must leave, and quickly. I will tell my parents and soon." She kissed him tenderly and got up to dress. When she had reached the place where her English transformation happened, she was saddened by the thought of leaving. She somberly adorned her Amish uniform and came out to meet Cade. He held her close, kissed her forehead, and without saying a word, he led her to the car. Their drive to pick John up was short, and before they knew it, they had pulled up in front of Kelly's house. Cade went to the door and knocked. Kelly and John came to the door with each one holding a child. Cade watched as they both walked to the car. Rebecca got out and met them in the middle of Kelly's yard. John said, "Becca, I would like for you to meet Kelly, and these are our sons Joseph and Jonathan." Rebecca looked carefully at each one and said, "Oh, John, they are beautiful! It is very nice to meet you, Kelly." Kelly smiled and said, "It is nice to meet you as well. John explained your situation to me today, and I hope that everything turns out the way you want it to. John will explain to you our plans. I also want to thank you for encouraging him to contact me. I prayed every day that he would. I am a different person than I used to be. I want the boys to be raised with a father and a mother, especially one like John." John wrapped his arm around her waist and kissed her forehead. "Everything is going to work out, just wait and see," John said as he handed her the baby in his arm. "I must go now, but I will call you tomorrow and let you know what my father says," John explained. Kelly shook her head and waved goodbye. Rebecca got into the car where Cade had already gotten back in. He thought that they may need some privacy to discuss their situation. When John came around to get in, Rebecca could see that leaving her was tough for him as it was for her to leave Cade. Rebecca turned back around and filled her fingers with Cade's hair. He kissed her hand and squeezed it tightly. When Cade pulled up at the bus stop, he whispered, "I love you, I will call at ten." Rebecca smiled, and she and John quickly got out of the car so as not to be seen. They sat in silence as they traveled back to the feed store. When they got there, the store owner was just locking the door. He tipped his hat at the two and left. Rebecca was the first to speak, "John, I am going to tell Mother and Father this week of my intentions. I am not going to ask permission either. I am going to *tell* them. I cannot stand being away from him. Today I was truly who I want to be. I also was with the *one* I want to be with." John was not surprised at the statement at all and said, "Well, I guess that we will both hit them this week because Kelly wants to come live with me. She wants to convert to the Ordnung. I am going to talk to the bishop, first I must get his approval, and although I asked forgiveness when I committed to the Ordnung, I want to clear this whole matter. I do not want to upset Mother at all, but this is too important." "Your situation is different than mine. You are making right a wrong that was done in rumspringa. I, on the other hand, am renouncing the Amish Church and the Ordnung." The rest of the trip home was made in silence. Both were lost in thought. They wondered of their future and what lay ahead.

CHAPTER 8

"Thank you for seeing me, even if unannounced, Bishop Miller. I have something that I need to speak to you about. I am really not sure where to begin. I guess I will start at the beginning. Senior Bishop, when I was in rumspringa, I met a girl. We dated for several months, and I fell deeply in love with her. I was later told by someone that she was seeing someone else and that she did not feel the same for me. I did not contact her from then on. That is really the reason I have not actively sought a wife. I had feelings still for Kelly, and I knew that I should not seek a wife until I had dealt with those feelings. I had already made the decision to commit to the Ordnung when I also found out that she was pregnant. I assumed that the reason she had not called me was that the child belonged to the other man she was seeing. Bishop Miller, I ran into the person that told me about the other guy and the pregnancy, and he informed me that he had lied. I went and had seen Kelly today. Senior Bishop Miller, I have two sons, Joseph and Jonathan. Kelly had twins. She wanted to contact me but thought I did not want to see her and really did not know how. I have asked forgiveness of all this when I committed. I need to know if it's possible for her to convert to the Ordnung and the Amish Church. She has researched on this a lot and is ready to do this. She and I are deeply in love and wish to raise the boys together," John said as he suddenly felt as though a weight had been lifted from him. Bishop Miller took a long breath and asked, "Have you spoken to your father?" "No, I have not, but I intend to tonight. I wanted to talk with you first. I respect my father and his wisdom, but I am a man. I can handle things on my own. I am going to my father whether you say it is possible or not. I did not come to you first with the intention of keeping it from my parents. They have not told anyone yet, and I am not sure that some of my brothers and sisters know yet, however, Mother is expecting again. After what happened with Annie, I am a little hesitant to cause any problems now. I have wasted time with my sons already. I do not wish to waste any more." Bishop Miller could see that John had given this a great deal of thought. He continued, "Has she spoken to her mother and father about this at all?" "Yes, she has, her father and mother, although they do not think she is ready for such a commitment because of the difference in lifestyle, they feel it is right for her to want to raise our sons with both of us," John explained. Bishop Miller thought a moment in silence and said, "Well, I feel that you have a valid reason for allowing her to convert. I am not making any promises, however, you talk to your father, and I will talk to the elders. I will see them tonight for our annual meeting. We will discuss this, and I will call on you tomorrow to let you know of the outcome." John shook his hand as he left and headed straight home. When he arrived, he found his father in the barn working on some plows that he would need for the harvest. "Father, I need to speak to you and Mother as soon as possible. Something has come up, and it is urgent," John urged. Samuel saw that whatever it was must be important and put his tools down and wiped his hands. He put his arm on John's shoulder and said, "I needed a glass of mint tea anyway!" Samuel arrived in the kitchen to find Mary was baking pies for their supper. The girls had not yet returned from an errand that she had sent them on. "Mary, John has something to talk to us about." Mary sat the bowl down and came to sit at the table. "Mother, Father, I committed to the Ordnung with a clear conscience and after having asked forgiveness of my sins. However, during my time of rumspringa, I met a girl, her name is Kelly. We dated, and I fell deeply in love with her. After some time, a person that I thought was a friend told me that she was seeing someone else at the same time she and I were dating. The same friend came to me right before I committed and said that she was pregnant by the other guy. I recently found out that all this was a lie. The only truth was she was pregnant but by me. I have seen her, and in fact, she gave birth to twins, both boys. I have two sons, Joseph and Jonathan." John pulled the picture out of his pocket. Although pictures were forbidden, this time it was appropriate. Mary's hand went over her mouth at the sight of the two precious boys. She had listened to everything that he had said and was not ashamed of him at all. "I have spoken to Kelly in length, and it is her desire to convert to the Ordnung. She had researched and studied on this for a while. She wants us to raise our sons together. She has her parents' permission, and I have spoken to Bishop Miller. The annual meeting is tonight, and he shall come by in the morning to let me know," John explained. "You have done the right things, son, and although I cannot condone your behavior during rumspringa, I cannot deny that I have two grandsons. My only question is what if the elders say no?" Samuel asked, almost not wanting to hear the answer. John looked at his father and mother and said, "I am not sure. I am certain that I want to be with my sons. I have wasted this much of a time that I have with them. I do not want to make the same mistake." "We have some news of our own, John, we have not said anything to the others yet, but your mother is expecting again," Samuel said, smiling. "That is wonderful, Father, and I hope that all turns out well," John said as he shook his father's hand and kissed his mother's cheek. "All my extra errands have put me behind in my chores, I must get to work. I do want to thank you very much for your understanding in this matter. I am very fortunate to have both of you," John said. He returned to his chores and worked extra hard for the rest of the day. He wanted to keep his mind off as best as he could and also to make the morning come that much faster. He had worked all the way till dark before he came in the house for supper. He walked to the front steps and saw Bishop Miller's buggy. He doubled his stride into the house and saw that he and his parents were seated in the living room. "John, we were about to think you were going to put kerosene lanterns on that plow horse and work all night. I have just returned from the meeting and thought I would drop by. I knew you probably would not sleep. They have requested a meeting with all parties. They wish that Kelly, her parents, the boys, and your mother and father to attend a special meeting Thursday afternoon. Do you think that is possible, John?" Bishop asked. John knew that her parents were due back in the morning; he could call them and see if they were willing in the morning. "They have been out of town. However, they are due back in the morning. I will go see her and see if it is possible," John said. Bishop Miller continued, "Well, let me know. I must be getting home." "Thank you, Bishop Miller, very much. You have no idea how much this means to me," John said as he walked him out the door. John washed up and came to the table where the family had gathered. When he had finished his meal, he told everyone that he was going to bed. John lay in his bed thinking about Kelly and his boys. He prayed that she would be able to adapt to the Amish way of life if they let her in. She was a simple girl, she had never worn makeup, and although she did wear worldly clothes, she never dressed in anything but jeans and a shirt. She had talked of a family and having a farm. She spoke lovingly of the grandfather that lived nearby whom she helped plant and harvest. He drifted off to sleep as he imagined life with them.

He was up and knocking on Rebecca's door very early. "Come in, John, how did it go?" Rebecca asked hastily. John explained, "The talk with Bishop

Miller went well. The talk with Mother and Father went even better. They have requested a meeting with all of us: Kelly, the boys, her parents, me, and mother and father. I need to borrow your phone to call her." "Sure." Rebecca went upstairs as John followed her. She got the phone from the lockbox in her closet and handed it to John. She closed the door behind her to allow John privacy. Her mind reeled at the thought of how well it was going for John. She hoped that her parents would take her news as good as they had taken John's. She thought if the subject came up on Friday on their way to the doctor, she might confide in her mother first. John came down the stairs as though he was floating on a cloud. "They have agreed, tomorrow afternoon it is," he said. "I gave directions to her father, and he is bringing them to our house after lunch. Please be there, Rebecca, I need your support in this. Besides, you can help Kelly with the boys if the meeting runs a while." "I would not miss this for anything, John, of course," Rebecca said as she gave him a huge hug and watched him walk out the door. When he returned to see Bishop Miller, he told him of the plan. They would all be at his house at two. Mary was in the living room sitting in her rocking chair. She was repairing some socks that had holes. She saw the smile on John's face when he walked in and waited for him to tell her the good news. "They will be here tomorrow at two!" Mary sat the mending down and hurried for the kitchen. "I will get busy making some pies and cookies for my little grandsons then!" John smiled at the thought of her being excited over her grandchildren. He could not wait until his boys were with him here. Although they were only one year old, he would love to have them by his side. The day crept by and, despite the hard work, would not pass any faster. When dark finally came, John rushed to bed in hopes that morning would arrive.

The morning did finally arrive, and John was elated. He paced the front porch as the time for them to arrive came. Rebecca came down the drive shortly after lunch and laughed at the sight of her brother. He was a nervous wreck. She hoped that the meeting would go well, and they were allowed to be together. She also wondered if they were not allowed, what his decision would be then. She tied her horse up at the tie post of the barn. It was under a huge oak and would offer Daniel's horse the shade it needed. She came to the porch to give her brother a hug to maybe calm him down. He heard the car slow down to turn in their drive. He could not help but think that was an odd sight. He could not remember the last time he had seen a car come up the drive. It came to a stop at the steps, and John went to greet them and help Kelly with the boys. He shook Mr. Douglas's hand

and welcomed him. Mrs. Douglas took in every detail of their house and could not stop talking about how beautiful it was. Samuel and Mary came out, and when they saw Joseph and Jonathan, their eyes filled with tears. They looked just like John. It was amazing. They greeted the Douglases and welcomed them. Brice and Martha Douglas knew how they felt and were very sweet in their response. "They had the same effect on us when they were born. They are precious little boys, and I must say it again, they look like their father. I am sorry how this whole thing came about, Mr. Fisher. Although I am not sorry that I have these two fine grandsons. I think John is an honorable man, and I think they are doing the right thing," Mr. Douglas told Samuel as he shook his hand. Mary invited them in where all the other children were sitting on the couch waiting to be introduced. John introduced them one by one, and to his amazement, Mrs. Douglas remembered their names. When they all were seated, Mary said, "I have some refreshments if anyone would like some." "Kelly, it is very nice to meet you. I am sure you are quite nervous but don't be," Mary added to try to calm her nerves. "Just be yourself and answer any of the questions with honesty and I pray that it will turn out the way we want it to. Do you feel that you are ready for a life such as ours?" Mary went on to ask. Kelly immediately looked her in the eye and said, "Yes, I am. I am sure this will be a drastic change for me. I also know that I will have days when I regret my decision because it is too hard. The only thing I can say is when John left, I was devastated. He was so different than the others that I dated. Whatever he said he was going to do, he did it, and I knew that I could trust him. I love him so much, and when he left, I knew there had to be a reason. I also knew during the whole pregnancy that if I could reach him that no doubt he would be there. I want to make this work so bad. I want to raise our boys together, and if there are more children down the road, well, I would love that too. I am willing to do whatever it takes." Mary saw her determination and her love for John. She had peace of mind that it was the right thing for them to do. When the elders arrived, Mary offered them refreshments, and they began to talk. The meeting lasted about an hour, and Bishop Miller and the elders came to the same conclusions. The only exception was that Kelly's parents could come for visits whenever they wanted. John and Kelly were elated at the news. Rebecca could hardly keep herself seated. She wanted so bad, while they were all there, to tell them of her news as well. If it had not been for Kelly's parents there, she would have. It was when her parents announced that they were leaving that she thought she might have a chance. John brought Rebecca out of her trance by saying, "Is that all right, Becca?"

When he saw the bewilderment on her face, he repeated the question. "Can I stay at your house tonight? Kelly wants to stay here and discuss wedding plans." "Yes, that is fine." When her parents walked the Douglases to their car, the elders and Bishop Miller were still eating their cake that Mary had gotten them. Rebecca spoke up, "May I have a chance while you all are here to discuss something with you?" The elders and Bishop Miller gave her their attention. "I would like to wait till Mother and Father are here before I speak," Rebecca said more boldly. Samuel and Mary came in with such sweet faces that Rebecca wished that she had not spoken already. However, there never was going to be a good time, and she might as well get it over with. "Mother, Father, while everyone is here, there is a matter I wish to discuss with you all as well." John's face went suddenly pale. He hated to do this to his parents although he was convinced that they were deeply in love and deserved to be together. "I recently met an Englishman. We have seen each other weekly since, and we are deeply in love. Although it breaks my heart to do this to my mother and father, I am going to marry him as soon as possible and live in the English world." The elders all gasped at her announcement. They could not believe that Rebecca would do such a thing. Samuel stood there in shock. When he came to his senses, he put a hand to the small of Mary's back to offer support if she fainted. Mary quickly took a seat and gripped the armrest on the chair. Bishop Miller was the first to speak. "Rebecca, how long have you known this man?" "It has been a little over a month now. I know what you're getting at, and you do not think that I have known him long enough to fall in love. I assure you that this I feel is love. I also am confident that he feels the same." Rebecca would not look at John for fear the look on their faces would give it away. She did not want to involve him in this. She did not want to mess up anything that had been done here today. Samuel spoke, "Daughter, you would shame your family like this." "I am not—" She was interrupted by John. She took a quick breath in because she feared what he would say. "Father, she has not shamed this family any worse than I have. The only difference was my wrongdoing was done in rumspringa. Rebecca married Daniel and would still be married to him if it were not for the accident. Did you know, Father, that she never loved him. Nor did Daniel love her. That is why she does not have children. Please find favor with her as you did for me." Rebecca had tears in her eyes as John finished. Samuel looked at his daughter and said, "Is this true, Rebecca?" "Yes, Father, it is. It was not long after we were married that we knew that the only feelings we had for one another was that of a sister and a brother. We had relations only a few times the whole time we were married. I would have stayed married to him. I am sorry I lost a friend, but I desperately wanted a chance to be happy. I am so sorry for hurting you, but I love Cade, and I am going to marry him." Rebecca watched as Bishop Miller and the elders whispered among themselves. She knew she was in the way and wanted to leave their presence anyway. She started to leave, stopping only to hug John and Kelly and congratulated them on their news. "Thank you, John, for all that you said. I love you." Rebecca's stride got quicker until she was in a full run. She hopped on her buggy and reined the horses as fast as it would go. When she got on the highway headed toward her house, she was crying hysterically. She was so upset and lost track of where she was. She was almost to town when she realized how far she had gone. She was turning her buggy around when a car came out of nowhere. When it hit her, the impact threw her from the buggy and onto the highway. The car came to a sliding stop, and the driver running to her said, "Oh god, miss, are you all right?" Rebecca suddenly became unconscious.

When a car started up the driveway, Samuel knew something was terribly wrong. It was when he saw that it was the sheriff's car that his heart sank into his stomach. The deputy got out of the car and said, "Mr. Samuel Fisher?" "Yes! Yes, that is me," he quickly replied. "I am afraid I have some bad news. Your daughter Rebecca was involved in an accident tonight. I am going to need you to come to the hospital right away," the deputy stated. Samuel could not think, his mind was reeling at the possibilities. The only thing that he was sane enough to ask was, "Is she alive?" The deputy said, "Yes, she is, but I am not sure of her injuries." Mary had come to the door just in time to hear the deputy. She had already gone into the house to get John when Samuel made it inside. "John, your sister has been in an accident. Your mother and I are going with the deputy. Please bring your buggy and meet us there." She has been taken to Calvert County. John did not have time to think. He kissed Kelly goodbye and headed to the barn. It was while he was hitching his buggy he thought about Cade. The only way he could think to get in touch with him was the cell phone. He hurried in the direction of Rebecca's house. He ran up the stairs and got the phone. He quickly called. "Hey, baby! I am so glad you called," Cade said as he expected to hear Rebecca. "Cade, this is John," John said while crying. Cade knew that something was wrong; he waited for John to explain. "Cade, Rebecca has been in an accident. She had been taken to Calvert County Hospital." "Oh god, NO!" Cade said. "I will see you there." John hung up the phone and hurried to his buggy.

When Samuel and Mary arrived, they walked into the room where Rebecca still lay unconscious. It was not long before Rebecca's doctor came in to talk to them about her condition. "Mr. and Mrs. Fisher, my name is Dr. Klein. Rebecca is stable, she has a broken arm. The only other thing is a very bad concussion. She took a nasty bump on her head when she was thrown from her buggy. Does she have a husband?" Dr. Klein asked. "No, her husband was killed in an accident a while back." He looked over his bifocal glasses and said, "So she is a widower then?" "Yes, she is," Samuel replied. Dr. Klein looked puzzled and walked away. Mary came to sit at her daughter's side. She kissed her hand and began to pray. When Cade got to the hospital, he raced to the nurse's desk. He asked, "Rebecca Lapp, is she—" "Cade! What are you doing here?" asked Dr. Klein. "Hello, Rodger, my fiancée just had an accident." "Is Rebecca Lapp your fiancée?" He looked at Cade with a questioning look on his face. "Yes, she is, Rodger, we have been seeing each in secret. I know how this may look, but she was going to tell her folks this week. What happened?" Cade asked. "She was hit by a car. She has a broken arm and a concussion. I think she is going to be fine," Rodger stated. Cade said, "Thank God, where is she?" Rodger pointed to the room and said, "Her parents are with her now." Cade brushed by him. "Cade, there is something else you should know," Rodger said in a hushed tone. Cade twirled around to see what he was going to say. "She is six weeks pregnant, and the baby is fine so far." His words rang in Cade's ear over and over. He was thrilled at the news but very worried about her condition. "Is there a chance that she could lose it?" Cade asked worriedly. "Yes, there is. Does she even know that she is pregnant?" Rodger asked. "I don't think so. She has not said anything to me," Cade replied. "Have you said anything to her parents?" Cade asked. "No, I have not." "Good, this is bad enough without them knowing about it right now. Thank you, Rodger, for everything," Cade said as he walked toward Rebecca's room. Cade walked in and introduced himself. "Mr. Fisher, my name is Cade Matthews." "You are Rebecca's fiancée?" Samuel asked. Cade could not believe that he knew about him. "Yes, I am," Cade said as he walked to the side of the bed opposite from Rebecca's mother. Cade took Rebecca's hand. He squeezed it lightly so as not to cause any pain from the broken arm she had suffered. He kissed it and held his face to it. He gently caressed Rebecca's face. Mary watched Cade in silence. She could tell that his love for her ran deep. She could also see the way he looked at her that they had been intimate. She was convinced of it. She hoped that her husband could not tell. His heart would surely break. He had had enough disappointment for one week. "I am sorry we had to meet like this. I know you have a lot of questions. I also know that you doubt my love for your daughter. I love Rebecca more than I have ever loved anyone. She and I are extremely happy, and I want to spend a lifetime that way. Time can only prove this however." Samuel motioned for Mary to follow him. Just as Mary rose to her feet, Rebecca began to stir. When she opened her eyes, the first person she saw was Cade. "Cade, what happened?" she whispered sleepily. "My angel, you are going to be fine. You were hit by a car." Rebecca fell back to sleep, and her parents left the room. Cade watched her breathe. He could not believe that she was having his child. He was so happy at the news. He just hoped that she would not miscarry. He stared at her stomach and envisioned the child that lay beneath.

When John arrived, he saw his mother and father in the waiting room. When he was close enough so that they could hear, he asked, "How is she?" Mary spoke first, "She has a concussion and a broken arm." John was relieved at the news. He could tell that his father was upset, and when he looked around the corner, he knew why. He was grieving for the daughter he was about to lose. "Mr. and Mrs. Fisher," Dr. Klein called. "The latest scans show no signs of brain swelling, I think she is probably out of the woods. However, I am not releasing her until she is awake and showing no signs of any problems." Mary shook her head and said, "Thank you, Doctor, so much for all you have done." Dr. Klein continued to walk to Rebecca's room where John had made his way. "Cade, the latest scans show no signs of swelling. I think she is out of the woods, but we will just see." "Thanks, Rodger, I am not leaving. So keep me informed," Cade stated. John quickly asked, "You know him?" "Yes, I do. We play tennis together sometimes. We belong to the same country club. John, thanks so much for calling me. I know that will probably be bad on you. I met your parents, and they are not happy at all. How did they know about me anyway?" Cade asked. "While everyone was still together earlier, Rebecca told all of them about you. She said that she loved you very much and that she was going to marry you and live among the English. I should have not let her go. She was quite upset, and I am sure that is what caused the accident," John stated. Cade could not believe she had told them all. He was so proud of her. He thought about the likelihood of him being able to bring her to his apartment after she was released. He could not wait to start their life together. He wanted to tell John the wonderful news of her pregnancy but decided to wait until she was able to join in the excitement as well. Samuel entered the room with a scowl on his face and said, "We have done all we can do. Your mother needs to go home and rest." John nodded and started in the direction of the door. "Cade, just give my father some time. He has had a lot thrown at him for the past few days. I think when he has had some time to think on this, he will come around. After all, the only difference between what she has done and what I have done is the time in which it happened." He patted Cade on the shoulder as he made his way to the door. When they had left, Cade realized that they were in fact leaving her to him. He was thrilled with the fact that he could sit with her all night.

It was right before daybreak when Rebecca came to; she looked around and began to process what happened. Cade said with a smile, "Hello, my love, I am so glad you are awake. How are you feeling?" Rebecca smiled halfheartedly and replied, "I am feeling queasy. My arm hurts too." Cade said, "Your arm is broken, and you have a concussion, but Rodger says you are going to be fine." "Rodger?" she asked. "He is your doctor. He and I belong to the same country club, and we play tennis together sometimes. Although I am sure that my time is about to be spent somewhere else." Rebecca smiled brightly at that and said, "Yes, I think so." She looked around and said, "Did my parents come?" "Yes, they did. Your mother held your hand, and your father and I met. I was shocked when he knew who I was," Cade explained. "How did you find out that I was here?" Rebecca asked. "John called me from the cell phone that I gave you." Cade was about to tell her the news when a nurse came in. He waited patiently until she had finished and gone. "Rebecca, I have something to tell you, baby," he said slowly. "Like I said, Rodger and I know each other well. When he found out I was your fiancée, he thought that I should know the dangers that you faced. Baby, did you have any idea that you were pregnant?" Cade watched as the realization hit her. Her hand covered her beautiful red lips, and her eyes filled with tears. "Oh, Cade, are they sure!" she said as she felt her abdomen. "Yes, angel, you are six weeks along," Cade said enthusiastically. "I am thrilled. I could not be happier," he said as he kissed her lips gently. Rebecca could not believe the news. She was so excited to be a mother. It was unreal! "I want you to know that Rodger said that everything looked good. However, the danger of you losing it is still there." Rebecca suddenly went somber. She hoped that everything would continue to go well. "Do my parents know about the baby?" she asked. "No, I knew you would not want them to know just yet. We will tell them together," Cade said as he rubbed her face. Rebecca lay still for a moment and drifted off to sleep again. Cade sat at her side and watched while she slept. It was right as the sun was rising that Rodger came in the room and handed Cade a cup of coffee. "I thought you might need this, Cade. I remembered that you drank it black," Rodger said. "Yes, thank you, Rodger," Cade responded. "I have ordered a pelvic ultrasound, and I am going to turn her over to an obstetrician. Her name is Wendy Goldstein. She is as good as they come, and I think Rebecca would be more at ease with a female obstetrician given her condition. I don't know how you two met, but this will be a wonderful story to tell your kids someday. My shift is over, but my replacement will be in shortly. If you need anything, just call my cell," Rodger explained. "Thanks again for all that you have done." Cade sipped on the coffee slowly as he looked out the window at the sun coming up. "Cade, I am very hungry," Rebecca said, startling him. "Well, I will see if I can get you something," he answered with a smile. When he returned to the room, he said, "They will be bringing you breakfast in a minute. I am so glad to see you have an appetite," Cade said as he lay in the bed beside her. He rested his hand on her abdomen and kissed her lips sweetly. They were interrupted by a knock at the door. "Good morning, you two, I am Wendy Goldstein, the obstetrician that Dr. Klein referred you to. Let me first congratulate the both of you on your little one on the way. Dr. Klein ordered an ultrasound for this morning, and as soon as you have eaten, we will get that going. Do either of you have any questions?" she asked. "Yes, I do," Rebecca said. "How long will it be before I am out of the woods?" "Let me run all my tests, Rebecca, and as soon as I get the results, I will be back in to talk with you about them." "Okay." Rebecca gave her a concerned smile and looked at Cade. When she had gone, Cade said, "Rebecca, I love you, baby. I want this baby so much, and if something happens to it, I will be greatly upset, however, we can get pregnant again. As long as I have you by my side, everything will be fine." Rebecca felt so blessed to have someone so sensitive as Cade. After Rebecca had eaten, they came to get her for her ultrasound. When they saw the little butter bean speck with its beating heart on the monitor, they both were elated. The technician said, "You will have something big to be thankful for this Thanksgiving because your baby is due late October. Cade kissed Rebecca's lips tenderly and said, "I love you so much. You have made me so happy." The technician smiled at the couple, and even her eyes filled with tears. They took Rebecca back to her room where they casted her arm and talked of her release. Rebecca was in a quandary as whether to go back to her home or go to Cade's. She wished she knew what her parents were thinking.

CHAPTER 9

Rebecca had drifted off to sleep when Cade woke her by kissing her forehead. "I am sorry to wake you, my love, but your parents are here to see you. I am going to give you some privacy. I am not going far, but I will give you some time." Rebecca was thankful that Cade understood her need for privacy. She did not want to lose her family entirely and hoped that a reasonable compromise could be met. When her parents came in the door, Mary came and kissed her cheek. "How are you, my daughter?" she asked sweetly. "I am better today, Mother, thank you," Rebecca said as she smiled back at her mother. Rebecca turned her gaze to look at her father, and she was not surprised to see a look of anger. "We might as well close this door and talk about this." "I am sorry for what I have done, but I am not sorry for loving Cade. I was not sure how to tell you because I knew that you would be angry, Father," Rebecca said, pleading. "You turned down a good man to run off with someone that is going to cost you your family?" Samuel said in anger. "Father, if you are referring to Ezekiel, he is not as good as you think," she said as she pulled the hospital gown down slightly to let him see the cut that still had not healed entirely. "What are you talking about, girl?" Samuel said as he took off his hat. "Father, the other day, Cade came to the market to see me. When I went into the room where my surplus is, Cade followed me in there. I did not know it, but Ezekiel saw us in an embrace. Ezekiel had already improperly made advances on me a few days before he saw us. He stopped by my tent as I was packing and wanted to apologize. He insisted that he gift me a settee as a token of his plea for forgiveness. When I gave in, he followed me home and dropped it off. I felt that I should at least show him as much and offered him something to drink. I was in the kitchen preparing it when he came in and tried to . . . *rape* me, Father! He is not as good as all that. You see things the way you want to see them and nothing past that. Please, I beg you get to know Cade. I am not asking you to love him. I am just asking you to give him a chance. I am going to marry him no matter what you decide about him. However, I love my family dearly, and I do not want to lose you." Rebecca finished with tears running down her face. Samuel gripped his hat tighter and sat somberly in a chair at her side. "Are you sure, daughter, that Ezekiel—?" "Yes, Father, I am. I have the torn clothes to prove it. This is not about him though, Father, and I do not wish for anything to be done about him. He will in time be the destruction to himself. I have forgiven him, and I harbor no bitterness toward him. I have done equally wrong, Father," Rebecca said, sobbing. Samuel heard everything she said. He had no idea though what she was implying by her last statement. He thought she meant that her rebellion was equal to his attempted rape. Rebecca's mother on the other hand knew exactly what she meant. Samuel wanted to wipe from his memory what he had heard. He did not want to believe that his judge of character had been wrongly placed in Ezekiel. He got up slowly and left the room. Mary, seeing Rebecca distressed, quickly said, "Rebecca, he will come around. Just give him time. Rebecca, I see that you are not telling the whole story. Please, daughter, tell me so I can try to help." Rebecca looked at her mother and, with tears running down her face, said, "Mother, I have given myself to Cade. We have been intimate several times. I am pregnant. I am very happy to be pregnant with his child, and I love him so much." Mary sat on the edge of her bed. "Rebecca, I must say that I am disappointed, but I cannot say that I am surprised. If you love this man and he loves you, then I am happy for you. I will speak to your father in private about this matter. Maybe I can make him decide to give this man a chance," Mary said quietly. "Mother, that is all I am asking. After all, did you not do the same thing for Kelly? It is because she wishes to covert to the Ordnung that she is more accepted. I am very happy for John, truly I am. I want this to work for all of us," Rebecca pleaded. Rebecca lay there as her mother comforted her.

Samuel needed some fresh air to clear his head. How in the world could his children have gotten so far off track? What should he do about this whole mess? He had sat down on a bench near the entrance of the hospital when he realized that Cade was standing nearby. Cade said, "Mr. Fisher, I am glad you are here, I wanted to talk to you in private, and I was not sure how to ask." Samuel saw that Cade was very serious and replied, "Well, Cade, it seems that I have been wrong about a lot of things lately. I will listen to you, however, do you wish to do it now?" "Yes, I do. I want to tell you that I understand how you feel about all this. I am not familiar with the Ordnung or the Amish way of life, but I know this is hard to take. It would be for any parent. I just want you to know that I love Rebecca very much. I have not dated many women because I wanted someone that loved me because of me. Mr. Fisher, I am a wealthy man and believe me when I say that I could have been married several times by now if I chose that. I was waiting for the right one to come along that would unconditionally love me. Rebecca is beautiful, she is honest, she is trustworthy, she is humble, and I could stand here all night and still I would not reach the end of what she is. I have never felt this way for anyone. I also know that she loves her family very much. I do not want to take that away from her. Please try to find it in your heart to forgive us for what we have done and let's all try to build a relationship for her sake. There is one other thing that I feel that you should know too. Mr. Fisher, Rebecca is pregnant with my child. I am sorry if this disappoints you. I do not regret any of this. I am however sorry that this might cause you shame. You may blame that on me, not Rebecca." Cade could see that Samuel needed time to himself. He stood there in silence for a moment, making sure that he had no questions for him, and then walked away. When Cade walked into Rebecca's room, he knew that she was very upset. He hated that it had to come to this. He wanted to take all the hurt from her. He took her hand and kissed it. "Your father and I had a talk, Bec. I hope that you will not be upset with me, but I told him our wonderful news." Rebecca was not upset; she was relieved that everything was out in the open. She hated lying, and this way, whatever happens, she could have a clear conscience. "Your father is a good man, Rebecca, he will do the right thing when he figures out what that is." When Samuel entered the room, he had done it in a manner that conveyed to everyone that he had something to say. "I have decided that I am going to talk to the elders and Bishop Miller about this. I will ask them to reconsider shunning. If this is going to work, that is the only way I can see that it would. If you want to live in the English world together, that is the only way. I also am asking you to marry my daughter right away. It is not proper for her to be unwed, furthermore, I wish that you do not speak of this pregnancy to your siblings until you are married and a proper amount of time has passed. I do not want them to suffer any ridicule because of it nor do I want to set a bad example for them to follow." Cade shook his head in agreement. "Thank you, Father, for understanding, I know this is not what you expected from me, however, I am not sorry that I fell in love with him. I love him deeply." Samuel walked over and kissed her hand and motioned for Mary that it was time to leave. Cade lay beside her in the hospital bed. He had a lot on his mind, and Rebecca was exhausted from all that had happened. He lay beside her until she fell asleep, thinking about what he should do. Later, when Rebecca woke up, Cade was gone. She lay there for a moment and decided to sit on the edge of the bed. She was trying to do that when she saw Cade at the nurse's station. She sat and watched as Cade came into the room with a wheelchair. Cade said with a huge smile, "Are you ready?" Rebecca was a bit puzzled about what he meant and asked, "Ready for what?" "Are you ready to become Mrs. Caden Thaddeus Matthews III?" Rebecca smiled at the thought of that and answered, "Yes, I am, but what are you talking about?" "When you fell asleep, I called Mother and enlisted her help with the arrangements. We have a minister and all the trimmings. They will be at the house at six o'clock this evening. I also have your wedding dress waiting for you as well. It will not be as grand as you might have dreamed, but we will be married just the same. What do you say, are you up to it?" Cade explained. Rebecca was speechless. She was so excited. "Yes! Yes, I am!" she said as she put her hands over her mouth. Cade wheeled her out of the hospital and put her into his car. Their trip to Cade's apartment was a short one. The moment she walked in to the door, there were people to help with everything. As everyone busied themselves getting her ready, Rebecca felt as though she was in a fairy tale. Cade had left, and she was sure what she was supposed to do next. When her hair and makeup were finished, Rebecca could not believe that the person in the mirror was her. This was the first time that she had ever worn makeup, and her hair was fixed more beautiful than it had ever looked. Cade's mother came in the room with a box and said, "Cade asked me to give you this." When she opened the box, it was the most magnificent dress she had ever seen. It was simple in design but still the most beautiful thing she had ever seen. When Gloria helped her put it on, it fit her perfectly. It was made of ivory satin. It was to her feet with a little draping of satin that flowed behind her. There was a beautiful blue satin ribbon at her waist. The bodice was very modest with a neckline that gave only a hint of what lay underneath; however, the back was cut so that most of her back was showing. She felt so beautiful that she thought she was going to cry. She realized that the blue satin ribbon accent was to match her eyes, just like the engagement ring. She had had it in her shoe during the accident and, as soon as she was able, had asked someone to get it for her. As she looked at herself in the mirror, she knew exactly what she wanted to wear for her jewelry. She went into Cade's room and retrieved the necklace and earrings he had given her. Gloria helped her put the necklace on, and as she put the earrings into place, she stared into the long mirror of the closet. She remembered the beautiful sandals that he had gotten for her and quickly put them on her feet. When Rebecca walked out into the living room, everyone was taken aback by her beauty. Gloria looked at her and said, "You are the most magnificent bride that I have ever seen, my dear. Cade is going to be speechless when he sees you." The doorbell rang, and when someone opened it, a lady holding this square box came inside. When she saw Rebecca, she said, "Madam, may I say that you are stunning. Mr. Matthews asked me to bring you this." She opened the box and pulled out a bouquet of beautiful blue irises all tied together with white satin ribbon. She also pinned a beautiful iris corsage on Gloria. Gloria said, "Well, my dear, are you ready to go?" Rebecca looked around the room and said, "First, I want to thank each one of you from the bottom of my heart. You have made this special day even more special by the kind things you have done. I feel as though I am a princess." Gloria could not believe her kind words. She was extremely touched by her sincerity. Rebecca got to the door, and Gloria motioned for her to get in. It was a long black limo with a huge blue bow on the top. Rebecca prayed silently that if this were a dream, she would not wake up.

They arrived at the farmhouse, and Rebecca's breath was again taken away at the decorations. There were tables of food everywhere. The driver pulled around to the back as he was instructed to do. Rebecca was brought up the back stairs to a room upstairs. When she was settled inside, she heard a knock at her door. Rebecca almost fainted when she saw her parents and John. She burst into tears at the sight of them. Samuel and Mary were not prepared to see the beautiful image in front of them. John was the first to speak. "Becca, you are too pretty for words. You look amazing." Mary was the next, "Rebecca, my dear, you are a sight. You are stunning, my dear." Samuel took a long look at her and said, "You look beautiful, my daughter. If you would have me, I would be honored to walk you down the aisle," Samuel said with a little hesitation. "Oh, Father! I would be honored if you would. Come inside, all of you." They chatted a few minutes about the house and all the arrangements. "I really do not know how he did all this in a matter of a few hours. When you left, I fell asleep, and when I had awakened, he had all this arranged. I am so lucky to have him," Rebecca said. Just then, they heard another knock at the door. "Come in!" Rebecca shouted. Gloria appeared with an iris corsage for Mary and a boutonniere for Samuel. Gloria turned to Rebecca and said, "If you are ready, the ceremony will start in fifteen minutes." Rebecca smiled brightly and said, "I am ready!" Gloria laughed and left the room. John and Mary decided they would go to their seats. Mary kissed her beautiful daughter's cheek before she left. Samuel and Rebecca were waiting for someone to come tell them it was time when Samuel said, "I have spoken to Bishop Miller and the elders. They will let me know in a few days of their decision." "Thank you, Father, I pray that they will do as I ask." When the knock came, Rebecca heard the music change. She was very nervous as they made their descent down the spiral staircase. She could hear the reaction of the people below and knew they were commenting on her. It was when she had reached the last step that she saw Cade. He was in a black suit with long tails. His vest was black as well with a light blue tie. He was so handsome. She could not help thinking how lucky she was. Cade was speechless. He had tried many times over the afternoon to envision her in her dress. Although he helped pick it out, he was not prepared for what was before him. Her beauty could not be matched. She was a vision of perfection. How lucky he was that she wanted him for forever. It was equally hard for him to believe that she was carrying his child. When she reached the end of the aisle, Cade stepped forward to meet her and her father. As Cade took her by the hand, he shook Samuel's hand and thanked him. When Cade and Rebecca approached the minister, her knees were trembling as she walked. Cade could sense her nervousness and put his hand to the small of her back. As the minister prepared to speak, Rebecca marveled at how the house had been decorated. There was greenery all over the railing of the staircase, and iris bouquets put in ever so often. There were two stands of candles in front of them with huge bouquets of flowers sitting everywhere. Rebecca was still amazed at how well it were decorated. When the minister started, her heart raced at the thought of her being Cade's wife. The ceremony began, and as they stood there pledging their vows to one another, Rebecca's heart raced wildly. Tears filled her eyes as Cade said his own vows. His words were so tender and precious that she could not help but cry. When it came for her turn, she was unbelievably not nervous at all. She spoke clearly from her heart, and when she was finished, Cade himself was wiping tears. When it was time for him to kiss his bride, he took Rebecca in his arms and kissed her tenderly. As their lips parted, he whispered, "I love you, Rebecca Matthews." Rebecca could not wipe the smile from her face. She stood proudly at his side when the minister announced them husband and wife. They ran down the aisle as the people cheered. When they had made their way onto the lawn, Cade grabbed her and held her tightly. The photographers were snapping pictures wildly. Cade took her by the hand and led her to the reception area. The tables were decorated impeccably well and, despite the quick response, were adequately supplied. When Rebecca got a look at the wedding cake, she was flabbergasted. It had four layers, and each one was covered with blue irises. The rest of the day went by fast, and Rebecca was sad to see her parents leave. They had been the first to leave, but she could not even believe they came. It was not too long before the limousine was pulling up to whisk them off for their honeymoon. When they were safely inside and pulling down the lane, Rebecca said, "That was the best day of my life! How did you pull that off in only a few short hours? My dress was absolutely beautiful! The flowers and the cake were gorgeous! And my bouquet—" Cade put his finger to those beautiful full red lips and said, "My mother can throw a party on a moment's notice. She actually did all the decorations and the food. I picked your dress and made arrangements for the people that were at the apartment. I have another surprise for you however." Rebecca could not believe her ears. She would surely wake up any minute now. "What is the surprise?" she asked, like a child on her birthday. "I will not tell you anything other than we have an hour or so before we get there." Rebecca looked out the window of the limo as if she could tell which way they were headed. When she was certain that she could not, she asked, "How did you get my father to walk me down the aisle?" Cade said with a smile. "Your father loves you very much. He was touched that I was so quick to do as he asked. He was also equally touched at the great pains that my mother and I went through to get this done. We wanted everything to be perfect for you." Rebecca quickly answered, "And it was!" She kissed him tenderly and snuggled in for the ride. Cade turned and retrieved a bottle of sparkling grape juice that was chilled, waiting for them. "I took the liberty of choosing this for us. I knew you probably would be thirsty, and you cannot have alcohol in your condition," Cade said with a devilish grin on his face. They chatted about the wedding and how it came to be. They also discussed plans for their new life together as husband and wife. When they arrived at the harbor, Rebecca was tingling with excitement. The limo driver got out and opened the door. Cade was the first to get out and grabbed Rebecca's hand. When she saw the ship in front, her mouth opened wide, and the most childish scream came from her that even she was amazed. Cade laughed loudly and said, "This is our honeymoon, my angel. Do you like it?" Rebecca put her hands over her mouth and marveled at the sight. She quickly hugged Cade, squeezing him tightly. "Cade! I cannot believe this!" Cade took her hand and led her over a small bridge that connected to a beautifully decorated yacht. It was covered with white lights and flowers along the railings. When they arrived on deck, there was a full crew waiting. They were prepared to serve a seven-course dinner by candlelight. Music was playing softly, and Rebecca loved it. "I called Rodger, and he did not think it was a good idea that you traveled by plane just yet, so I settled for a yacht. Although we are not setting sail, I didn't think that a tossing boat would be good for morning sickness either," Cade explained. "Cade, this day has been wonderful. I will remember it always. It has been perfect!" Rebecca boasted. "I do have one request however," she said timidly. "Anything! The sky is the limit, my beautiful bride," Cade said loudly. "I would love for you to teach me to dance," Rebecca asked with a smile. Cade took her into his arms and began to lead. Within minutes, she looked as if she had been doing it all her life. "I see you are a quick study. Let's see if I can spin you a little," Cade said boastfully. He twirled her around gently a few times, and she squealed with delight. Rebecca was floating on a cloud of fairy dust. When Cade thought the expectant mother had had enough, he led her to her seat. They enjoyed a delicious meal. Rebecca had finished her food and walked to the railing. Cade instructed the crew to leave when they were finished with the cleanup and not to disturb them down below. Cade danced with her once again and, this time, held her so close to him that she was sure he would smother her. "Rebecca, there are no words to describe your beauty. You take my breath away, baby. I hope this child is a girl and hope she is as stunning as her mother." Rebecca kissed him tenderly. She kissed him so gently yet so seductively. Her eyes conveyed to his soul that she was in need. Without a word being said, Cade whisked her off her feet and carried her below. The room was filled with candles, and the flickering flames matched the passion that had been ignited between them. Cade set her down gently and took one more look at his beautiful bride. He stepped away to allow her to undress. When she turned for him to unzip the lovely gown, she could feel Cade trembling. She let out a hot breath as he moved her hair to rest on one side of her neck as he kissed the other. He wrapped his hands around her waist and began to rub her full bosom. Rebecca began to whimper. As Cade unzipped the delicate dress, he kissed her spine. It made Rebecca's body tingle with delight. The beautiful dress fell to the floor, and Rebecca turned to face him. She wore a blue satin bra and panties. Cade drank in her beauty. Rebecca released her hair, and it fell in loose ringlets on her face. Cade removed his jacket and loosened his tie. When he started to unbutton his shirt, Rebecca pushed his hands away and began the process. When his black matted chest lay before her, she kissed the patch seductively. As her trail took her lower and lower, Cade threw his head back in the wonderful agony of what was to come. Rebecca watched as Cade ran his fingers through her beautiful long tresses. His fingers were covered with her blonde ringlets as she slowly began to take his belt off. She unbuttoned his pants and slowly kissed the trail that led to his swollen manhood. Cade bit his lip as she slid her hands onto her pants to remove his trousers. She squeezed his tight buttocks and felt the rock hardness of them. When the pants slid to the ground and his throbbing member was revealed, she slowly began to stroke it. Cade was surprised at her boldness. She had never shown this seductive side to him before. It was driving him mad. Even now as she took his shaft into her mouth, he was planning his revenge. The feelings that came over him were breathtaking. She was delighting him fully. Cade could not take it any longer. He lifted her to her feet and began to kiss her full voluptuous breast that threatened to burst out of the barrier at any moment. He ran his tongue up her neck and unfastened the blue satin material, and it fell to the floor. Cade watched as her bosom danced in delight at being released. He watched as she licked her lips; her mouth had suddenly gone very dry. Cade lifted her swiftly and carried her to the bed. The bed was already rolled down, and the satin sheets had been sprinkled with rose petals. Cade kissed her and said, "My god, how I love you, Rebecca." He looked into her eyes and in unspoken words that spoke of its depth. Rebecca surrendered her body to him once more. She could not believe the passion that he could invoke in her. He slid the tiny piece of delicate satin from her, and when he entered her, it was if someone had poured hot coals on both of them. Their passion was reaching all new heights. Rebecca heard sounds coming from her that she had never made before. Cade watched as she fought the flames of the hot fire. He loved this woman more than life, and even now, she was branding his soul. She had given him all her untold gifts that only lovers know of each other. She had boldly surrendered all her secret desires. Cade knew that her release was near. He thrust himself into her and felt her release. He too joined her as they exploded into the clouds. Both of their bodies jerked violently from their release. When they were able to speak, Rebecca said, "I love you, my husband." Cade took her into his arms and held her lovingly. He was at peace knowing that she was the completion of him. He had searched for her all his life, and it took him twenty-six years to find her.

CHAPTER 10

When the sun peaked through the blinds, Rebecca could hear the gentle lap of the water as it kissed the vessel good morning. She could believe that she was waking up as Cade's wife. She positioned herself to watch him sleep. She had only gotten comfortable before he said sleepily, "Good morning, Mrs. Matthews, did you sleep well?" Rebecca smiled and answered, "Yes, incredibly well. Thank you." Cade massaged her beautiful body. He could not stop wanting her. He watched as his gentle massage delighted her. The sight of her hair flowing around her in disarray and those perfectly pouted red lips that had begun to part in her anticipation of what was yet to come made his body ache. Cade slid his hand to that dark blonde matte that lay beneath him. It was when he touched the special womanly place that brought her the most delight that she let out a loud moan. His manhood was threatening to burst at the very sound of it. He mounted her and began to gently enter her. Her body quivered with the force of it. He made love to her tenderly, enjoying every treasure that her body held. Cade's body was overtaken as his thrusts became faster and faster. Rebecca, matching his rhythm, knew that her release was near. She clung to him desperately as they both floated to the heavens once more. They both lay sated and completely fulfilled as the heat of passion left them. Cade kissed her softly and asked, "Are you hungry, my darling?" Rebecca wrinkled her nose and said, "Famished!" Cade got up and handed her robe. It was lying on a chair nearby. She quickly wrapped it around her and sat on the bed; Cade had done the same and crawled back into bed. Rebecca was a little puzzled but followed suit. Cade rang a small bell that was on his nightstand. Within a matter of a second, the intercom came on and a lady said, "We will be right there, Mr. Matthews." Rebecca was amazed when they tapped on the door and brought a table that was perfectly set and with beautiful fresh cut flowers. There was another table carted in behind them with several silver-covered dishes and a pitcher on it. On one side were two coffee carafes. Rebecca smelled the delicious food and admired how beautifully it was prepared. When the attendants had left, Cade took Rebecca by the hand and led her to her seat. Cade shoved her chair in and took his seat as well. She lifted her cover off her plate and followed Cade's lead. Her coffee cup was already filled, and she gently set it aside. Cade smiled and said, "It is decaf, my love. I took the liberty of requesting that for you. I did not think you would object." She smiled at his thoughtfulness and fixed it to her liking. They shared small talk and ideas for the day. Rebecca said, "I really want to call your mother and tell her thank-you for all that she did. I am still amazed at how quickly that was put together. I am sure that must have cost a fortune." "When you compare it to a lifetime of memories, it was relatively cheap. I wanted to make it as special for you as possible. I want to make all your dreams come true," he said as he came to kneel by her side. "Rebecca, you have made me the happiest man in the world. I love you deeply, and there is nothing that I would not do for you." Rebecca kissed him gently and caressed his handsome face. She admired how beautiful he was and how willing he was to make her happy. She truly felt blessed. Cade kissed the palm of her hand as he again seated himself back in his chair. "What would you like to do today, sweetheart?" asked Cade. Rebecca was excited about her new life and thought of a million things that she would love to do at her new home. "Cade, would you think I have lost my mind if I wanted to go home. This had been the best time of my life! But I also am looking forward to setting up housekeeping, and I would love to cook you dinner. I must confess that I am really just a simple person. I don't require all the fineries of life, although this has been the most incredible time of my life!" Cade could not believe his ears. She could have asked for the moon, and he would have taken her there, but she chose home. He was deeply touched. He was quite a homebody himself. "Rebecca, if that is what you wish, then that is what we will do. However, if you wish to sleep there, we will have to go bed shopping first," Cade said laughingly. "We don't have to, we can spend the rest of the day there and then go back to the apartment," Rebecca replied. "Okay then, we will get dressed and leave immediately." The limo picked them up and brought them to Cade's apartment. They picked up Cade's car and drove the rest of the way themselves. When they reached the lane, Rebecca could not believe that it was as if there had never been a wedding. They had not even left a crumb of cake. She replayed the whole thing in her mind. She could not help but wear a huge smile on her face. "What is that smile for, my darling?" Cade asked as he squeezed her hand.

"I was just remembering the best day of my life! I shall treasure the memory forever," she answered. They spent the afternoon there and shared decorating ideas and planned their moving-in party. Cade asked, "Which room is going to be the nursery, baby?" Rebecca blushed at the thought of it. Cade rushed to her and kissed her lovingly. He placed her in his arms so that her back was to his chest and kissed her neck as he gently rubbed her stomach. "I really cannot believe this, Bec! We are here in our new home, married, and now we have a child on the way. I am a very lucky man. I cannot tell you enough," he said as he faced her toward him and cupped her face in his hands. He kissed those ruby red lips so tenderly that she thought she would melt into a puddle of water. "Now, Mrs. Matthews, where would you like to go?" he whispered. "Anywhere as long as you are with me." Cade captured her lips once more; however, this time, his kiss conveyed his undying passion for her. His tongue searched her mouth with such tenderness that Rebecca's body was covered with a chill. As he trailed kisses down her neck, the wonderful mixture between hot and cold tortured her wonderfully. Rebecca sighed as her body surrendered to his touch. Cade began lifting her shirt slowly, as he lifted it, he kissed the naked skin that was revealed. When her bosom was exposed and he saw the beautiful full mounds that were barely hid from the delicate lace that held them, he lingered in the valley that lay between them. As he finished removing the shirt, he was quick to return to the piece that held these magnificent mounds captive. Upon their release, he ached to give attention to those pink peaks that stood to attention. While Cade still squeezed and kissed her, he lifted her from her feet. He carried her to the soft carpet and gently laid her down. He removed the rest of her garments and stood in awe at the sight of her beauty. He began to undress, never taking his eyes off the woman who lay at his feet. The look of passion was heavy on her face. Her wet, parted full lips beckoned him to her. Her beautiful crystal blue eyes were now a smoky gray as a sign of her passion. When Cade stood before her unclothed, she drank in the beauty of him— his shoulder-length shiny black hair that framed his incredibly handsome well-chiseled face. She watched as his blue eyes flickered with flames of desire. He towered over her with broad shoulders that led to a rock-hard chest that was matted with black ringlets. His waist led to firm hips that delivered her much pleasure. Rebecca watched as his hugely swollen manhood throbbed with the need of her. When Cade closed the distance between them, he once again tasted her sweet lips. He began to search for that wonderful spot that made her a woman. When he found it, Rebecca whimpered uncontrollably. He continued to stroke the hot, wet place that gave her pleasure. Rebecca's body was moving to the rhythm of his strokes; the intensity of her pleasure was in full view. She looked into his passion-filled eyes and said, "Take me, Cade, I am on fire!" Cade lifted her so that she was spread before him on all fours. He entered her forcefully with his hard shaft finding its place at the bottom of the honey-laded well. The intensity was so great and wonderful that Rebecca screamed passionately. Cade lifted her to him so that her back rested against his broad chest. He placed his hands around her tiny waist and thrust himself into her over and over. He wanted to savor this feeling as long as he could. He decided to slow the rhythm and once again bring her to intense pleasure. As his slow, gentle thrusts were delighting her fully, Cade wrapped his fingers with her blonde tresses and pulled her back to him. He kissed the small of her neck and tingled with the taste of it. With one hand, he captured her breast that danced with each thrust. He was amazed at the intense passion that they shared. Cade whispered with a breathless voice in her ears as he held her tightly, "I love you, woman! My body craves for you, Rebecca." Cade continued once more to forcefully thrust his aching member that threatened to explode with each plunge. The complete pleasure that Rebecca felt was quite evident. She could not help the sounds that were escaping her. "Cade! I love how you bring my body to life! I love you, Cade!" She moaned seductively as her body jerked at the intensity of her release. Cade could feel her womanly place squeeze his manhood in gratitude of the pleasure that it was giving her. He held on tighter as he too found release. When they were floating to the ground, he laid her gently beside him on the floor. He kissed her face and lips as their breathing returned to normal. "Oh my god, baby!" Cade said, still breathless from the intense lovemaking. Rebecca smiled and replied, "Mmmm, yes! You are a wonderful lover. It is amazing how you make me come alive. Never have I known such intense complete pleasure." Cade kissed her again in gratitude. "I have never known such as this either, my darling. It really is as though we were made for one another." They lay there for a while before they attempted to get up. Cade held her close as he drank in her aroma.

When Rebecca woke up the next morning, she could not believe how queasy she felt. She tried to lie still to get some relief. Cade was just getting out of the shower, and when Rebecca raced past him to get to the sink, he realized what was happening. He quickly got her a cold cloth and held her hair as she heaved over the sink. When she was all finished, he walked with her, and she crawled back into bed. He sat and watched as the color came back to her face. He held her hand and tried to comfort her. He quietly said, "I will get you some fresh ginger today. I can make you some ginger tea, and maybe that will help ease your morning sickness if you continue to have it." Rebecca shook her head in agreement. When Rebecca was feeling better, Cade took her out on the balcony for some fresh air. He had fixed them a quick breakfast of bagels and juice and carried the tray for them to enjoy it outdoors. Cade knew when Rebecca finished her bagel in two bites that she was feeling much better and said, "Were you hungry, my love?" The realization of what he was implying hit her, and she laughed at the unmannerly way she had eaten her bagel. "Well, as a matter of fact, I was," she answered, wrinkling her nose. When the phone rang, Cade answered it, and when John was on the other end, Cade knew it must be important. He handed the phone to Rebecca. "Rebecca, it is Mother, we are at the hospital. Mother lost the baby!" John said in a broken voice. "Is Mother all right?" Rebecca asked. "Rebecca, she is bleeding badly, and the doctors are trying to stop it," John replied. Rebecca said, "I am on my way!" Rebecca got to her feet so fast that she got dizzy. She grabbed the railing to try to steady herself. Cade was at her side in an instant. "Bec, what is the matter?" Cade asked worriedly. "My mother is in the hospital, she lost the baby, and they can't seem to stop the bleeding," she said while she held her temple and the railing. "No, honey, I mean with you," Cade reiterated. "When I stood up, I suddenly went dizzy. It is getting better." Cade swept her off her feet and carried her to the sofa. He laid her down and sat beside her for a moment. "Cade, I have to get to the hospital," she said as she was about to cry. Cade caressed her face in his hand and said, "Bec, you are my first concern. I will get you to the hospital, but I want you to see Dr. Goldstein today too. You have looked a little pale the last few days. Are you sure there is not something going on that you have not told me about?" "No, baby, I promise. I am feeling much better, may I get a shower now?" Rebecca said, smiling. Cade answered, "Yes, but I am coming with you. I do not want you to fall." He held her hand so that he could grab her if she were to fall. Rebecca was amused at his way of hovering over her. She was touched however. She showered as Cade sat patiently nearby. He watched as she washed herself. He cursed himself that now even in sickness, his body still ached for her. He could see the beautiful curves of her body and tried to think of something else. When she had gotten out safely and seemed to be steady on her feet, he got in the shower after her. Rebecca slipped her jeans on and could not help notice they were a little snug. She watched as Cade washed his beautiful body. Rebecca looked in the mirror and wondered about her father's reaction to the way she was dressed. Cade quickly dressed, and they left for the hospital. When they arrived, John was the first person they saw. "How is mother?" Rebecca asked. "Father is with the doctor now. He will be out shortly." Rebecca grabbed Cade's hand and held it tight. She was not feeling well again but did not want Cade to know. When Samuel came out, his face was pale, and he looked as though he had seen a ghost. Rebecca sucked in to brace for bad news. Cade saw the look on Samuel's face too and wrapped his arm around her waist in support. Samuel walked grimly and said, "They cannot stop the bleeding. They are getting her ready to take her into surgery. It is up to God to save her now." Rebecca burst into tears. Cade held her as she cried uncontrollably. He knew that she would blame herself for her mother's illness, and if she died, he was not sure if she would ever overcome it. John patted his father's shoulder to show support. Samuel was beside himself. When the hospital door opened and Mary was wheeled out on a gurney, Rebecca got up and kissed her mother. Cade stood behind her, comforting her as best he could. The family watched their mother as she disappeared through the double doors. Rebecca had a feeling like she would never see her mother alive again. She forced the tears back because she knew that is not what her father needed right now. She also knew that the baby she was carrying was her responsibility, and she did not want anything to happen to it. When Rebecca had stopped crying, Cade said, "Honey, let's go to the cafeteria and get you something to eat. If we go now, we will be back in time for some news." Food was the last thing on her mind right now, but she knew she needed to eat for the baby. She grabbed her purse and asked, "Father, can I bring you anything?" Samuel shook his head no. Rebecca could not take her father looking so heartbroken. She walked over and sat beside him and said, "Father, she is going to be all right. Mother is a strong woman. God will see her through this." She hugged him tightly to her and kissed his cheek. Samuel looked into Rebecca's crystal blue eyes that were the exact color of his own. He wanted to believe that so much. He also knew that he should not have taken Mary that night. He indulged himself in his own pleasure. If Mary died because of his fleshly needs, it would be hard to live with. Procreation was the only reason for intercourse. He knew this and should have abided by it. He sat and thought about himself and his children. It suddenly dawned on him that he had done the exact same thing his children had done. He had given in to lust. How could he punish Rebecca for the same thing that he had done.

 Rebecca forced herself to eat. She was feeling a little queasy and decided it was because she had an empty stomach. As she ate her salad, Cade asked, "Rebecca, are feeling guilty because your mother lost the baby? I know you well enough to know that you would blame yourself for this." Rebecca could barely hold the tears back. She composed herself and answered, "I do feel partly to blame. I feel that the situation with me and John probably did not help. The Amish belief is you are not supposed to be intimate unless you intend to have a child. My father took my mother when they were not trying to have a child. When Annie was born, it was a very difficult delivery. They couldn't stop the bleeding then either. The doctor begged my father to allow him to do a hysterectomy on her then, and my father would not hear of it. I fear that if my mother does die, that my father will blame himself for the rest of his life. So you see, I am only part of the reason. If father blames himself, he will also blame John and me as well." Cade now understood the situation better. He understood how this could end up as the ruination of this family. He hoped that it would not mean the ruination of his as well. "Rebecca, please try to keep from getting upset. I know this is your mother and your family but think of our baby and your own health as well. I do not want to face life without you either," Cade said as he swallowed the lump in his throat. He kissed her hand and held it to his face. Rebecca tried her best to smile, she was trying to be brave and silently prayed that her mother would be all right. When they had finished their meal, they headed back to where the family was gathered. Rebecca brought several cups of coffee and began handing them out. She handed one to her father. They sat for hours waiting for someone to give them word on Mary's condition. It had been three hours since they had wheeled her back when the doctor came from the double doors. Samuel got up and met him halfway of the hall. "We have done the hysterectomy, and the bleeding is at a minimum. If everything stands like it is now, she is going to be all right. We had to give her a considerable amount of blood, and we are not out of the woods completely yet, however, I am going to keep her sedated for twenty-four hours and let's just see what happens." Samuel shook his hand and thanked him. "We are taking her to intensive care for the night, Mr. Fisher. I will let the family see her for a moment and then you may see her again in the morning." Samuel shook his head in agreement and walked to where everyone was standing. "They have not stopped the bleeding completely, but the surgery is over, and it has slowed. They are going to take her to intensive care tonight. We will only get to see her for a moment and then again in the morning." Rebecca hugged her father and said, "See, I told you she was a fighter. She is going to be all right." When they came as a family and were led to where Mary was, Rebecca could not stand to see her this way. She sobbed quietly as her mother's frail body lay before her. Cade hugged her tightly and said, "The worst is over, baby, just hang in there." When they ushered the family out, Samuel said, "John, I am not leaving. I am going to stay here tonight. I feel it is best that you go home and be with Kelly and the children. If there is any change, I will send for you." Rebecca had already began to say that she was going to stay too when Cade intervened. "Rebecca, our apartment is only twenty minutes from here, I will give my number to the nurses at the desk, and if there is any change, they will call us. I really feel that you should at least try to rest." Rebecca knew that was the best thing, and she offered for her father to come there to stay as well. When he declined, she understood and hugged him goodbye. Cade patted him on the shoulder and wished him a good night. The drive back to the apartment was a somber one, and Cade knew that she needed some rest. When they pulled into the garage, he said, "I am going to call the nurse's station and make sure they have my number, baby, you go ahead and get a shower." Cade called, and Mary was resting and stable. When Rebecca had gotten out of the shower, she came into the kitchen in one of Cade's T-shirts, her hair was wet, and it hung in wet ringlets. Cade fought a war with his body. He knew that Rebecca needed some sleep, and the last thing she needed tonight was him harassing her. "Everything is fine, baby, and she is stable." Rebecca grabbed a glass of milk from the refrigerator and drank it down thirstily. Cade watched as her full bosoms bounced under the T-shirt. He wanted to tell her how beautiful she looked but was afraid that she would take that as a hint for sex. She smiled and kissed him gently. "I will be ready for bed in a moment," she said as she made her way down the hall. Cade decided to get a shower before crawling into bed, preferably a cold one. He lay beside her holding her tight as she quickly fell asleep. Cade was up the next morning before daylight. He knew that Rebecca would want to go the hospital as early as she could. He cooked breakfast, being careful not to wake her. He wanted her to sleep as long as she could. He arranged her breakfast tray with food as if he were a famous chef. He wanted it to be perfect. As he walked into the bedroom, he could not help but admire her beauty. He loved the way she looked with her hair lying on the pillow in disarray. He sat the tray on the nightstand beside the bed and began kissing her pouty full lips. "Good morning, my angel!" he said playfully. Rebecca wiped the sleep from her eyes and stretched lazily. She smells the wonderful aroma that lingered in the air. "Something smells really good. Oh! I need to call and check on Mother." Rebecca suddenly said as she was more awake. "I already did, love, she is fine, and they have started weaning her off some medication. I wanted you to have a nutritious breakfast, so I got early and prepared it for you," Cade said as he sat her tray in front of her. "Cade! Thank you so much, you are so good to me. This looks so good!" she said as she kissed him sweetly. She immediately started eating and got a sip of her coffee. "I knew you would want to get to the hospital as soon as you could, so when I could not sleep, I decided to get up and cook. I do hope you like it," Cade said as he shoved food into his mouth. "Mmm, yes, it is delicious," she replied. Rebecca was a bundle of nerves. She hoped today would be the day that there would be good news about her mother. She was also thinking about how hectic their life had been since they were together. She hoped that soon they would be in their new home with all the dark clouds that seemed to loom over them gone. She wondered if Cade regretted his decision to get involved with her. When they reached the hospital, Samuel was waiting outside in the hallway. Rebecca hugged him and handed him a cup of coffee that they had gotten for him on the way in. Samuel was anxious to see Mary. He had thought of her all night and hoped that he would find her much better this morning. He felt as if his whole family was falling apart, but if he lost Mary, he knew that it would never be the same. When it was time, they all walked to her room. When they got to the doorway, they could see that she was asleep and looked much better than she had the evening before. Samuel bent down beside her and kissed her forehead. Mary opened her eyes and smiled at him. She looked and saw Rebecca and held out her hand for her to come near. "I am going to be fine, Becca, please do not worry about me. You have your own little one to worry about," Mary said in a weak voice. Rebecca kissed her face and said, "I am fine, Mother, I knew you would be all right because you are a fighter." Samuel and Rebecca both were very glad to see that she was awake enough to talk and had improved greatly overnight. When the visit was over and they had made it back to the hallway, Samuel said, "I think I am going home to see to some things, and I am going to ride back with John this evening." Rebecca shook her head in agreement. "That is fine, Father, they have my cell number, and if anything should change, we will come get you. Try to get some rest before you come back," Rebecca said as she kissed his cheek. Cade and Rebecca left the hospital feeling much better about her mother. Cade was relieved for many reasons, most of all because now Rebecca could finally get some real rest and they could get on with the rest of their life.

CHAPTER 11

Rebecca was looking so forward to moving into her new home. The movers were going to be there in a few days, and she was trying to get as much stuff as she could into boxes. Cade had wanted to hire it done, but Rebecca told him that she could do it. He had made her promise that she would not work too hard or pick up anything heavy. She was extremely glad that her mother was home and doing so well. John and Kelly had gotten married. She had given them her house and had overseen the movers getting her stuff. She left the furniture and furnishings; all she had taken were the few things that had sentimental value to her. She had boxed all of Daniel's family heirlooms, and John returned them to his mother. John and Kelly were thrilled with their new life and home and had settled in quite nicely. She had gone to visit them and loved the sight of Joseph and Jonathan running around. It seemed so natural. Kelly had adjusted to the Amish life and seemed really happy. She especially loved seeing John with his boys. He was a wonderful father, and the boys had fallen in love with him. She caught herself wondering about Cade. She was certain that he would be a wonderful father. She could not wait till the baby came. She was lost in her daydream when Cade came in the door. When he kissed her neck, she screamed. "Oh, baby, I am so sorry, I really thought you heard me come in. Are you okay?" "Yes, I am fine, I was lost in thought," she said while holding her stomach. Rebecca turned and gasped suddenly. He looked down and saw her stomach was jumping with movement. He suddenly realized that the baby was moving for the first time. He quickly put his hands on top of hers, they could feel the life that they had made moving boldly for the first time, and both were brought to tears of joy. When the twirling frenzy was over, Cade caressed Rebecca's face and kissed her lips tenderly. He could not help but see how beautiful she was. The little pooch that was forming gave the only inkling to her condition. It was when the kisses turned more intense that Cade's body began to ache for the need of her. Rebecca sucked in a breath when he began to kiss her neck. He swiftly lifted her off her feet and carried her to their bed. When he placed her beside the bed, he began to undress her. Rebecca let her hair down from the knot on top of her head. Cade slid the shirt off over her head. When Rebecca pulled the latch on the front of her delicate undergarment, Cade could not help but notice how much fuller her bosom had become. The rosy peaks were darker now as they prepared for what was to come. Cade kissed the fullness as he pulled her to him. He slid the shorts and panties down and revealed her full beauty. He kissed the tiny bump that began to form and smiled at her sweetly. "You are beautiful, Rebecca! I honestly am amazed at how beautiful you are. I love you, baby," he whispered. He trailed kisses down to her dark matted spot. Rebecca let out a long breath as he teased her. He wrapped both hands around her hips and pulled her to him. He kissed the inside of her thighs until her breathing had become labored. She moaned with excitement. Cade sat on the edge of the bed pulling her on top of him. When his manhood touched her, the heat of it sent a feeling of hot passion all over her. When it entered her, she leaned forward to brace herself from the force of it. Cade captured one of the dark peaks and began to suckle. The pleasure that Rebecca was feeling was sheer bliss. It was when Cade lifted her and pressed her gently up against the wall that Rebecca could not contain the pleasure she felt any longer. He entered her again and plunged deep inside her warm, wet womanly place. Rebecca watched in a mirror that hung on the opposite wall at the force his hips were delivering this wonderful feeling to her, and she could not contain the heat that was consuming her. She dug her fingers into his back and began to moan loudly. Cade knew by the way her body tensed that she had reached her climax with much intensity. He wanted to delight her further and sat her down gently on the bed. He once again kissed her neck passionately. Although Rebecca had just floated from the heavens, her body was reeling with the need of him again. Her hips moved to show him that she wanted more. Cade entered her again, and this time, he slowly began his delightful rhythm. Rebecca clung to him desperately as the thrusts became harder and harder. Just as she soared once more to the heavens, she knew that Cade was taking flight as well. He captured her full lips and tasted their sweetness as they reached the heavens together. Cade loved this woman fully. She had completed him in every way. He had never before experienced such joy and complete pleasure as he had found with her. The passion they felt during lovemaking was a precious gift that very few ever find. He continued to kiss her sweet lips and caress her enchanting body as they lay there in the aftermath of the sweet love they had made. Rebecca was the first one to get up and got in the shower. Cade watched as she bathed herself. He was certain that he would never get enough of this woman. He decided to join her, and when he stepped in the shower, Rebecca could see that he was not through with her yet. As the warm water ran over their bodies, Rebecca was brought again to the wonderful place that only moments ago had left. Their bodies shook violently as their release came. Cade held her to him, enjoying her wet naked body next to his. He bathed her, and although no words were spoken, their hearts were speaking a language all on their own. Rebecca stood still as he dried her wet body. He watched as once again her picturesque body was hidden from him. Rebecca lay across the bed as Cade dried himself. He lay down beside her and held her close as they both fell asleep.

When they woke up, the evening sun was peaking through the bedroom window. "Rebecca, I have a surprise for you," Cade said as he gently rubbed her. Rebecca smiled and curled herself around her pillow. "What is it?" she said with a huge smile on her face. "I want you to pack a bag, we are leaving in the morning, and we will be gone until the weekend. Don't worry too much about clothes because you will not need too much, and we will buy those there." Rebecca could not believe this. "Cade, we are going to move this weekend. How can we leave?" Rebecca asked. "When we get back, everything will be done. I know you are going to want to move things around a bit, but we will do that Monday. I do not want you to do any of this. You are pregnant, Rebecca. Even if you were not, I still would have hired people to do that for us. I want to show you my favorite getaway place," Cade said as he caressed her face. Rebecca could not believe how incredibly lucky she was. She was sure that she would be spoiled from now on. "Okay, deal! But you have to tell me where it is that we are going," she said teasingly. Cade quickly replied, "Somewhere warm and sandy." Rebecca was sure that he meant the beach but thought that it would be somewhere around the spot they went on their honeymoon. Cade packed his bag while Rebecca prepared them dinner. She had adapted to the modern appliances well, and Cade was amazed at what a wonderful cook she was. He marveled over her baking, comparing it to some of the best chefs in the world. As they ate the wonderful meal, they talked of their trip, and Cade delighted in teasing her about the location. The next morning when they woke up, Rebecca dressed in shorts and a summer tank top. She had grown quite accustomed to the worldly clothes and was amazed at how much cooler they were. She loved flip-flops and probably wore them too much. She painted her toenails and was extremely proud of herself at the skill in which she had done it. She had tied her hair up with some cotton ribbon and was checking herself in the mirror when Cade came in the bedroom. "My god, Rebecca, you look great! How did you pick the perfect outfit without a clue as to where we are going?" Rebecca smiled sweetly at the complement and replied, "Well, it was just an accident because I really do not have any idea other than maybe a beach." Cade laughed loudly. He gathered their bags and loaded them into the car. When they were well on their way, Rebecca was a little confused because they were going in the opposite direction that she thought the beach was. When they started being in the airport, Rebecca could not hold her excitement any longer. "Cade, are we going by plane?" she said, giggling like a little girl. Cade never said a word but just smiled mischievously. When they took a turn behind the airport that led to a private hangar, Rebecca was still not aware of what was going on. All this was very foreign to her, and she was clueless. Cade drove up to a small airplane. When he got out and came around to her side, he said, "Welcome aboard, my love!" Rebecca's heart began to race at the thrill of it. She had never ridden on an airplane before and was not sure that she wanted to. The fear must have shown on her face along with the excitement. Cade took her chin in his hand and said, "Do not be afraid. My pilot Michael has been with my family for twenty years, we have gotten in some storms before, and he has always got us home safely. He knows that he is carrying the most precious cargo that I have, and he is the best," he explained and kissed her lips tenderly. He wrapped his hand around her waist and began to walk up the stairs to the doorway. Rebecca turned to see about their bags and noticed a man had gotten them and was following them up the stairs. She smiled and spoke and removed the hair from her face. "Cade, this is yours?" she asked in awe. "Yes, baby, this is ours," he replied. The idea stunned her. When they had reached the top of the stairs, the crew was standing just inside the doorway. "Michael, Joana, Kirby, this is my beautiful wife, Rebecca. Rebecca, this is Michael that I told you about, and Joana and Kirby are the attendants that have been with me for about a year now." Rebecca smiled and shook each of their hands. She greeted each one by their name but could not help but have this little butterfly in her stomach at the sight of the women. She thought both of them were very beautiful and could not believe that Cade had not seen that before. She wondered if he had ever dated either of them before. Cade held her hand as they came into the plane. She was amazed at how beautiful it was. She had never been this close to a plane before, let alone been inside one. She thought how ironic it was that now she owned one. She would be sure to tell John that one. He would laugh for days. Cade gave her a tour and brought her back to her seat. The attendants closed the door, and within minutes, the plane was moving toward the runway. Cade showed her how to buckle her seat belt and when he had done so sat beside her. He held her hand to reassure her that everything was going to be okay. Cade explained to her what would happen during takeoff and tried to answer any questions that she had. When the plane lifted off the runway, Rebecca had to remind herself to breathe. She was very scared, and she suddenly felt the need to relieve herself. Cade watched her as the plane lifted off. He could see how scared she was. He wondered if he had done the right thing. He was about to remove his seat belt to be nearer to her when a smile erupted across her face. He laughed loudly. How brave she was, he thought, even when scared to death, she could smile in the face of danger. Rebecca watched out the widow at Cade's back as the clouds billowed around them. When the bell rang for the seat belts to be removed and Michael came on and announced they had reached cruising altitude, Rebecca jumped and said, "That is good, right?" Cade kissed her slowly and said, "Yes, baby, everything is wonderful. I love you so much, Rebecca!" Rebecca felt as though she were going to melt. She kissed him tenderly as he put his hand on the back of her head to bring her closer to him. When Cade had finished, she noticed the women smiling at their embrace. When they had approached them to offer some refreshments, Joana asked, "Cade, can I get you some champagne or some other drink perhaps?" Cade smiled. "No, not this trip, I see that Michael forgot to tell you that Rebecca and I are going to have a baby. She is due in October. We are so thrilled, and I am elated at the thought of becoming a father. The baby moved for the first time this week, and I am blown away every day I spend with this woman. I am truly the luckiest man in the world," Cade said as he kissed Rebecca's beautiful lips again and again. Rebecca could not wipe the smile off her face. She quickly responded, "No, it is I who is the luckiest woman, never have I been happier than I have been these past few months." The ladies were almost in tears at the display, and Joana was the first to speak, "I am so very happy for both of you. I wish you the best in your marriage and your upcoming arrival. May I offer you something else then? We are stocked with almost anything." Rebecca gratefully declined as well as Cade. When they had walked away, Rebecca whispered that she needed to go to the restroom. Cade quickly got up and brought her to the bedroom where his private bathroom was. He showed her how to use it and sat on the bed to give her privacy. When she had finished, she saw the bed and thought it to look really inviting. She seductively captured his lips in a passionate kiss. Cade loved her boldness, and it excited him greatly. She started to undress him, kissing every inch of his exposed skin. When she had removed his clothes, she knelt between his legs. His hard, throbbing shaft was wet with anticipation. When Rebecca licked the droplet of juice that threatened to escape, Cade grew mad with passion. She began to stroke the huge member as she continued to tease it with her tongue. Cade put his hands in her hair as her rhythm became faster and faster. Cade felt his self-control leave him when he exploded in her mouth. The taste of the hot, salty treat that was filling her mouth sent her passion over the edge. She licked the member as it quickly became hard once more. Cade lifted her and laid her across the bed. He lifted her shirt to expose the beautiful bosom that lay beneath. He forcefully removed the shorts and threw them on the floor. He licked her peaks that were tingling from the heat of his breath. He nibbled them gently. He continued hot kisses until he had reached the wet patch that brought her so much pleasure. He stood over her, teasing the tiny bulb that became swelled at his touch. He watched her as her hips moved back in forth. Her passion-filled eyes watched him, and her beautiful full red lips were parted and glistened with moisture. He kissed the inside of her thighs. As he got closer to the spot that begged for attention, she began to pull him to her. He licked her as she moaned with ecstasy. Her body was on fire, and she knew that her release would not be far away. She quivered at the hot passion that he had created. She pulled him up and invited him inside of her. He plunged his shaft deep into the heated, wet well and began to thrust over and over. She lay beneath him, receiving his manhood, each thrust bringing more pleasure than the last until she burst into the heavens. He felt her body jerk violently as her release came, and he chased her to the heavens. Rebecca lay breathless under him as they both regained their composure. "I love you, baby!" Rebecca whispered. Cade covered her mouth with the most tender of kisses and said, "Oh, my precious Rebecca, it is I that love you from the depths of my soul." He lay on top of her for a moment. He felt tiny little thuds as the baby played underneath him. He kissed her stomach and delighted in the wonderful moment. He showed her where all the supplies to clean up were and waited patiently for her. When they were finished, they returned to the outside quarters. They had not realized that almost two hours had passed while they were in there. The attendants had the table set and welcomed them. They served them a delicious lunch as they sat and talked of their destination. It was sunset when they reached Cozumel, Mexico. When the plane touched down at the small airport, a limousine was waiting to take them to where they would be staying. Cade marveled in the reaction that Rebecca had shown. It reminded him of when he was a child at Christmas. He loved that he was able to experience these "firsts" with her. These moments were, after all, priceless. When they had reached the beautiful house that would be their home for the next few days, Rebecca could only sit in total awe. It was something out of a dream. After pulling through a private entrance, the driveway opened to this superbly landscaped lawn with palm trees and some sort of the most magnificent flowers that she had ever seen. In the middle of the circle drive was a fountain that had a picture of a mother and child on it, and the water flowed onto a pond with floating white flowers in it. The main house had huge pillars in the front with terra-cotta-colored paint and dark mahogany wood shutters. It was covered in a green running vine that covered the front of the lattice porch, making a cozy welcoming entrance. When the limousine stopped and the driver opened the door, Cade grabbed her hand and led her inside. The huge mahogany doors led to the foyer that was breathtaking. It had a huge black wrought iron and crystal chandelier. The staircase was directly in front of them that led to a black wrought iron balcony that looked down over the foyer. The living room was filled with all sorts of greenery and small trees. The windows were all open with large mahogany shutters that were held in their position by a large wrought iron pole. This allowed the ocean breeze to flow into the huge open space. The large French doors led to a magnificent veranda that even in midday would offer shade from the plush vines that grew there. There was a table that sat in the middle of the veranda that was set with brightly colored dishes, and candles were the only light. When they entered, an older Spanish woman welcomed them in broken English. Cade spoke to her in Spanish, and she nodded at the command he had given her. She motioned for Rebecca to follow her and up the stairs they went. When she entered the master suite, there were candles lit everywhere. There was a huge porcelain, claw-footed bathtub that had been filled with precisely the right temperature of water for her bath. The Spanish woman began to help her undress and, when she saw Rebecca's protruding belly, smiled and rubbed it gently as she muttered something about bambino that she could not understand. Rebecca crawled into the warm tub of water and delighted in the smell of it. The aroma of it seemed to wash relaxation all over her. She did not even mind it when the woman began to bath her. When she was done and Rebecca had let the water soothe her body, the Spanish woman held a warmed towel for her to wrap her wet body in. When she was wrapped sufficiently, the woman gently patted the remainder of her exposed skin with another warm towel to remove tiny droplets of water that remained. When the woman disappeared for a moment, she returned with several yards of material that had huge fuchsia and white flowers all over it. She gently removed the towels and quickly arranged the fabric on her body so that one shoulder was bare and the other was draped with the fabric. She let her hair down and gently began to brush it with a huge soft brush. When all the tangles were gone, she arranged her hair up and was pleasantly surprised of what it looked like in the mirror. She placed a beautiful fuchsia and white orchid behind her ear and adorned her feet with sandals that were made of seashells. Rebecca felt as if she were the most beautiful woman on earth. The lady led her back down the stairs where she found Cade staring at her at the bottom. He had on a pair of flowing white linen pants and a white silk long-sleeve shirt. She thought he was the most handsome sight she had ever seen. When Cade saw her walking down the stairs, he lost his breath at how stunning she was. When she was near the bottom, he climbed to meet her and took her hand and kissed it softly. He wrapped it around his arm and escorted her to the veranda. There were two Spanish men dressed in black pants and starched white shirts. They greeted her with broad smiles. Cade sat her down and pushed the chair under the table for her, once again kissing her hand softly. She watched a waiter poured them a glass of what looked like to be wine. Cade said softly, "A few sips is not going to hurt you or the baby. I talked to Dr. Goldstein last week to ask her if it was safe that you flew here with me. I told her of my plans, and she gave us both the go-ahead for a few sips tonight only." Rebecca was touched at the detailed manner at which he had planned this whole thing. The last remnants of the sunset were just fading, and if the sunset was this gorgeous, she could hardly wait till she could see the sunrise. When the waiter had filled both of their glasses with wine, Cade rose his glass, and she followed suit. "To our wonderful future and my stunning wife," he said as he butted his glass against hers. Rebecca took her first sip of wine. She loved the taste and could feel a hint of heat, even with the small sip, as it floated all the way to her toes. She smiled brightly at her beautiful husband. She could not help but feel extremely proud of his good looks, his long straight black hair that shined with the light that the candles made. She also noticed that the buttons that were undone teased her with the matted, rock-hard chest that lay underneath. She blushed at the tingling she felt between her legs and licked her lips at the thought of what the night would bring. "Cade, may I say how handsome you are. I am so very proud that you are my husband. I hope this baby has your looks, my love," Rebecca said provocatively. Cade could feel his manhood swell at the way her body language spoke to him. He felt almost silly the way his body was reacting. He also knew that Rebecca knew what she was doing to him, and the thought thrilled him greatly. She had become bolder in her intimacy with him, and it drove him mad. She looked beautiful, and the material looked as though her breasts were going to burst out at any moment. He could also see that the waiters were having a hard time keeping their eyes off her. The sting of jealousy ate at him, and he thought he would show them that she was his. He knelt on one knee and pulled something from his pants pocket. When he held it up, it was the most breathtaking pendant that she had seen since the blue diamond necklace he had given her right before they married. It was a white gold chain with a huge pear-shaped diamond hanging from it. "Oh my god, Cade, it is beautiful! Oh, baby, you shouldn't have done this, but it is so beautiful." She sat still while he placed it on her neck, and then he grabbed her right hand. He pulled a small black box from the other pocket and opened it for her. She could not believe that he had bought such expensive gifts for her. She glowed in the beauty of it. He slipped the matching pear-shaped diamond ring on her right hand and stared at how well she wore them. He lifted her up so that he could easily access her lips and kissed her passionately. The intensity in which he had kissed her surprised her greatly. She even wondered if he were going to dismiss the waiters and take her there. When he had finished, she was certain that she was blushing from the heat of it. She reached for another sip of the delicious wine. She felt light-headed, and her cheeks where hot. Her womanly place was also throbbing, and if she had her way, she would go to their room right now and she would make passionate love to him. When the waiters left them for a moment, he put his hand on her knee and slowly rubbed the inside of her thigh. When he heard them approaching, he removed it and stared into her eyes that flickered with flames of desire. The waiters set their food down, and Rebecca had to calm herself a moment before she could eat. She did not want to disappoint Cade and not enjoy all the wonderful plans that he had made for her. She finished the first course and took a sip from her water glass. The waiters removed their bowls and left them once again. This time it was Rebecca that kissed him passionately and sucked at his bottom lip while she felt for the swollen shaft that she longed to feel between her legs at this very moment. The approaching footsteps told them that that their second course was on its way, and Rebecca left Cade with lips that stung with her aggression. When the waiters sat their plates down, they smiled in courtesy and stood while they enjoyed their food. Rebecca tried to calm herself by listening to the waves of the ocean crashing against the sand. Cade could see the fire that burned slowly in her eyes. He wanted them to enjoy this dinner together and knew that he should try to behave himself. "Are you enjoying your meal, my sweet baby?" Cade said huskily. "Yes, I am very much, but the sweet lips that I just tasted are far better," she said very seductively. Cade could not believe her boldness, and he ached at the thought of it. When the meal was finally over, and he told the waiters to complement the chef, Cade clapped his hands, and a man walked out of the shadows and began to play beautifully romantic melodies on his guitar. Cade stood and said, "Will you dance with me, beautiful woman?" Rebecca smiled at her princely husband. She put her hand in his and loved how her body felt against his. They had danced for a while when Cade said, "Excuse me, one moment, my love." He stepped over to the man and said something in Spanish to him, and the man strongly agreed to whatever it was that Cade told him. He lifted her off her feet and carried her up the stairs as the servants cheered and clapped. Rebecca looked at Cade longingly as he hurriedly carried her to their room. Once inside, he gently placed her on the floor and walked over to the French doors that led to their balcony, and Rebecca could hear the guitar player as he played softly underneath them. She did not know if it was the wine, the atmosphere, or the ocean, but one thing was for certain, her body cried from the need of him. He unbuttoned his shirt and slipped it off, and Rebecca had done the same. She let the soft fabric fall to the floor. When Cade came to her, he said, "Rebecca, you are mine. I cannot bear that other men look at you. But I cannot blame them. You beauty is within and on the outside." He kissed her forcefully and continued down her neck. The harshness of it left her stinging, and this thrilled her. "You are mine, woman, do you hear!" he said as he thrust inside of her. He turned her back to his chest and claimed her breast in his hands as he thrust his manhood into her. They both watched themselves in a full-length mirror in front of them. Cade had never taken her this forcefully before. His jealousy still stung like a knife, and he had to prove to her she was his. He nibbled at the nape of her neck, and Rebecca loved it. She whimpered loudly as his passion burned her soul. Cade teased her womanhood, and he plunged his shaft deeper and deeper. He rubbed his hand over her as if he was claiming a war prize, he let his hand rest on her stomach, and he suddenly realized the harshness he was taking her. He went ghostly white and stopped. "Rebecca, have I hurt you? I am so sorry, baby, GOD! Please, are you all right?" He gently picked her up and laid her on the bed. She was not sure if she wanted him to stop what he was doing but certainly understood why. "I am fine, Cade, please don't stop. I understand what you are feeling. I felt the same thing today on the plane when Joana and Kirby were staring at you. That is why I had to have you and make love to you so boldly. Have you ever slept with either one of them?" Rebecca said, almost crying. Cade was amazed that he understood how he felt. "NO, baby! I have not. I am so sorry. I saw the way those waiters were looking at you. Your beautiful breasts were delighting them greatly and your gorgeous face. I could just imagine them undressing you and thinking what it would be like to bed you, Rebecca, I am so sorry, are you sure that I have not hurt you?" Rebecca answered, "No, sweetheart, I am fine. Please make love to me and wipe this from your thoughts. It is you that I love more than anything else in this world, and it is only you that I want touching me. Cade, you must know that," she said, pleading with him to understand. Cade kissed her tenderly and responded, "Rebecca, you know that I have searched for you all my life. You are the most caring, genuine, loving, gorgeous woman that I am madly in love with. I am so happy that you are carrying our child, and the sight of that takes my breath still. I am sorry if I hurt you in any way, darling, I do love you so." Cade kissed her passionately; he wanted to finish making love to her, but this time it was not going to hurt. He wanted it to be straight from his heart. He made mad, passionate love to her till dawn, and then they sat on the balcony and watched the sun come up wrapped up together in a sheet. When they watched the magnificent sunrise, they crawled into bed and exhaustingly fell asleep in one another's arms. It was lunchtime when Cade opened his eyes. He quickly replayed the events of the night before as he watched Rebecca sleep. He should have never taken her so crudely. If anything had happened to her or the baby, he would never forgive himself. He could not believe that jealousy had made him react that way. Any man could not resist the treasures that Rebecca possessed; however, if he caught them looking today, he would surely fire them. Rebecca began to stretch lazily in his arms. When she opened her eyes, she was unsure where she was; as the memories from last night began to flood her mind, she smiled at the wonderment of it. She could hear the waves crashing on the sand. She squeezed Cade and kissed his matted chest. "Good morning, my baby, I slept so wonderfully in your arms," she said as she rolled over, and the covers allowed one of her full breast to be exposed. Cade could see her little stomach that seemed to grow with each day. He lovingly rubbed it and kissed it. "Good morning, my child," he said in a funny voice. Rebecca laughed at the sweetness in which Cade was speaking. She felt the stone at the neck and was quickly taken back to last evening when Cade presented her with this stunning gift. She raised her hand and admired the diamond that sparkled in the midday sun. "Oh, Cade, these are so beautiful, baby! I know these were incredibly expensive though. I did not think that you could outdo the set you gave me before, however, these come pretty close," Rebecca said, still admiring the gift. "Rebecca, do not worry about money, my darling. We have more than we will ever spend," Cade said as he kissed her ribs and stomach softly. The reality of that was overwhelming to Rebecca. She still really did not understand the true meaning of that. Rebecca got up and wrapped the sheet around her. She went and stood on the balcony and looked at the beautiful teal blue water. She had seen pictures of this in books that she had gotten from the library but never dreamed that she would someday visit this place. Cade watched as she stood at the balcony railing, her beauty was breathtaking. Her beautiful long hair was being tossed by the ocean breeze. Cade came and stood at her back; he was showing her landmarks of the island when he caught a glimpse of one of the waiters. He was staring at Rebecca in a way that made his blood boil. He made his love for her known as he spun her around and kissed her lips longingly. "If you will put your robe on, my darling, I will let them know that we are ready for our lunch." Rebecca smiled wickedly and smiled as though she had been really bad. Cade admired the full red lips as they blew him a seductive kiss. He waited till she was out of sight from the waiter before he jerked the sheet from her playfully. Cade watched as her beautiful body glistened in the midday light. "Bec, would you like to go play in the water for a while after we have eaten." "Yes!" she excitedly said. "I am not sure if I have the proper clothing for that however." Cade went to her closet and pulled the bathing suit that he had handpicked from the many outfits. He walked into the dressing area and said, "This is only one that I picked out for you, baby." Rebecca loved it and could not wait to put it on. She had never been that naked in front of people and was a little uncomfortable thinking about it. However, she was sure that would fade. Rebecca put her robe on, and the waiter brought them their lunch. It was served on the balcony and consisted of food she never had before. When they had finished, Cade said, "Baby, while you dress for the beach, I am going downstairs and handle some business. I won't be far, okay?" Rebecca came out of the dressing room and smiled sweetly and said, "Yes, my darling, that is fine." Cade quickly put his clothes on and walked downstairs. When he saw the older Spanish woman, he spoke to her in Spanish and told her of the waiter that could not keep his eyes off Rebecca. He told the woman to give him his pay through the week and dismiss him. He wanted him replaced by evening with someone who could respect all that was his. The older woman shook her head in agreement and walked away. Cade returned upstairs and found Rebecca still in the dressing room. He decided that he would go to another bathroom and dress for the beach. Rebecca loved the bathing suit that Cade had picked for her to wear today. It was two pieces, and she laughed at the sight of her protruding stomach. Her full breast filled every inch of the fabric of the top without any to spare. She pulled her hair in a ponytail to one side of her head and braided it. She folded the braid and attached a beautiful scarf that matched her cover that he had chosen for her as well. She placed the sandals on her feet that had also been chosen and picked her bag that already was filled with things she would need at the beach. She could not believe how thoughtful Cade had been to see to her every need. She looked out at the beach and noticed the two waiters who were putting up a hammock and a table with refreshments on it. She watched as the Spanish woman walked to the one waiter and handed him something. He seemed to be really upset and stormed off. She did not hear Cade as he came in. He wrapped his arms playfully around her waist and kissed her cheek. "You are getting really good at that, Mr. Matthews," Rebecca commented. "Well, I am not sorry that I cannot seem to stay away from you," Cade said. "Cade, is everything all right? Why is the waiter upset?" Rebecca turned as she looked him in the eyes. "I fired him, Bec. I will not have anyone working for me that doesn't know their place. No one will ever disrespect you in my presence and get away with it. I overlooked last night, and then I caught him staring again this morning while we were on the balcony together. You are with child, for God's sake, Rebecca," Cade said in anger. "None of this is your fault, my love. The realty company should screen their employees more carefully," Cade said. Rebecca could understand him being upset and thought his decision to be wise. "Let us go and play, my beautiful wife! You look good enough to eat, and I cannot blame any man that is mesmerized by you, however, he better not let me see it," he said as he kissed her full bosom. Rebecca took his hand and followed behind him as he led her onto the beach. Rebecca quickly took off her cover and asked Cade to help her apply her sunblock. She laughed at the thought of how white she was compared to the dark skin of the Mexican attendants around her. Cade watched as she played just like a child that was at the beach for the first time. When she was tired of the sun, she came and lay with Cade on the hammock. She looked into the magnificent blue sky as the hammock gently rocked back and forth in the breeze. "Rebecca, are you enjoying yourself, my angel?" Cade asked. "Yes! Cade, I love it here. It is so peaceful, and I think I could stay here forever. I can certainly see why you love it too," Rebecca said, smiling. "What if I told you that I had made my mind up to buy this place and we could spend as much time here as we wanted," Cade said, watching her expression. "Oh my god, Cade, are you serious! I would love it! It would be an incredible place for our children to play although I would love to learn Spanish and teach it to our children," Rebecca said enthusiastically. Cade loved her so much, and his every thought was about what would make her happy. "Okay then, my darling, consider it done. Do you like Maria enough to hire her permanently?" Cade asked. "Yes, I like her every much, she was very sweet to me last night. What does *bambino* mean?" she inquired. "It means *baby* in Spanish, why, baby?" Cade asked. "Last night when she undressed me to bath me, she sweetly rubbed my stomach and said *bambino*. I thought that is what it might have meant. She was very sweet, and I loved it!" Rebecca explained. Cade kissed her lips tenderly; he could not express in words or actions how much he truly loved her. She was everything to him. Rebecca got up and chose the cold refreshing piña colada that had been made-to-order without alcohol. She handed Cade his and watched the sun kissed the waters that glistened with delight. They lay in the hammock all afternoon, and when the sun was beginning its descent, Cade decided it was time to dress for dinner. The two of them walked back to the main house arm in arm. When they reached the foyer, Cade said, "Baby, I am going to make some phone calls, go ahead, I will be up later," Cade explained as Rebecca continued going up the stairs. She was delighted when she entered her room to find the claw-footed bath had once again been filled to her liking. This time she soaked for a long time before Maria came in the room. Maria carried a large pitcher filled with warm water that would rinse her hair a. Rebecca loved the way the aromatic water felt as it brushed her skin. She especially loved the way it felt when Maria washed her hair. When she had finished, Maria once again held out her towel, and as Rebecca got up, she wrapped it around her. Maria went to her closet and picked a beautiful blue silk dress—it was strapless and allowed room for her protruding waistline. When Maria laid it on the bed, she knew without a doubt as to why Cade had chosen it. Maria started brushing her hair; she once again draped her hair to one side and started pinning her hair elegantly on her head. Maria then returned to the closet and brought out a pair of silver sandals that were trimmed in blue silk as well. Rebecca loved the way the dress felt against her skin. She could not help but think that she was the luckiest woman on earth. When Rebecca came downstairs, she saw Cade leaving the study with a stranger. When she started her descent down the stairs, the gentleman saw her and immediately stopped in his tracks. He spoke something in Spanish. Cade went to the bottom of the stairs and took Rebecca's hand and kissed it gently. "My god, Bec, you are stunning!" he whispered. He began again in Spanish, and the older Mexican man came and greeted her. "Senorita Matthews, may I say that your beauty far outweighs the heavens. Let me also congratulate you on the bambino that soon will arrive. Never have I seen such a beautiful woman, Senor Cade," the Mexican man said. "Yes, I truly am blessed," Cade said as he wrapped his arm around her. The men shook hands, and Cade bid him good night. "It is done, my love, you are now the mistress of the house. You may request anything, and it will be done," Cade said proudly. Rebecca put her hand over her mouth to keep from screaming. When she was finally able to speak, she said, "You are spoiling me, my love. I am presented with all these gifts, and I also am able to go back home and live in our new house there as well. I am so happy, Cade! But please do not think that I require all of this, baby. If you love me, I will be the luckiest woman alive," Rebecca said with a huge smile on her face. Cade wrapped her arm in his, and they went to the formal living room for tonight's dinner. Rebecca noticed the new waiter who smiled sweetly but never let his gaze stay on her for too long. Cade had watched carefully, and he was pleased with Maria's selection. "I have chosen two more attendants for you, my love. I have also inquired about a nanny for us as well. I know you are not the kind of mother that will hand her child over to someone else to be cared for. However, I thought that when we are down here and you wanted to go shopping or we wanted a day together that she would come in handy. She will really be valuable when we have more than one child to demand all our attention," Cade explained in detail. Rebecca was grateful and knew exactly what he meant. She had to help her mother with each new arrival. She cooked, babysat, and did all the cleaning whenever her mother brought home a new baby. "It is very demanding, and I am quite experienced with that as well. I am very thankful for the experience that I have gained, however, I will not be green when our baby gets here," Rebecca said as she kissed Cade in gratitude. "Bec, I need to go into town in the morning to attend to some business. Would you like to go with me and maybe do some shopping, or would you like to stay here and go to the beach?" Cade asked. "I would love to go into town and see all that they have to offer," she answered. "The business that I have will not take very long. We will spend the day looking at the sights if that is what you wish," Cade said as they began their meal together. Cade told her some of the things he wanted to show her and told of Cozumel's rich history. He also began teaching her some Spanish so that she would recognize the words if they were spoken to her. They finished their wonderful meal together, and Cade took her on a tour of the gardens as they made their way to the beach. Cade had made a place for them to sit and had requested that tiki lights be set up for them as well. Rebecca sat on the blanket and removed her shoes. Cade loosened his tie and took his coat off. He draped it over Rebecca's shoulders as the night ocean breeze was cool. "Cade, this is the most beautiful place in the world. Please don't show me anywhere else. I am happy to be here, and I will be torn when we are to leave it," Rebecca said as she laid her head on his shoulder. "We can come back as often as you like, and after the baby is born, we can come stay here for longer periods if you like." "Cade, I want to talk to you about something. I would like to give birth at home. I do not want to have our child born in a hospital. I have attended my mother giving birth many times, and I want to do that as well," Rebecca said with seriousness. Cade could see that she had given this a great deal of thought. He was quiet for a moment and then said, "If that is what you wish, then that is what we shall do. However, I want to search for a midwife or a doctor that will come to be with us. I do not want anything to go wrong without someone knowledgeable with us. Are you sure this is what you want, sweetheart?" Cade asked cautiously. "Yes, very sure, I want to discuss this with Dr. Goldstein next week when I go visit her. I will continue going to her for checkups, and we will find someone that will come to be with us for the birth," Rebecca said. Cade kissed her sweetly and replied, "You never cease to amaze me." He captured her mouth and kissed it tenderly; he laid her back on the soft blanket that had been so carefully laid there to protect them from the sand. Rebecca's breathing had become labored at the anticipation of what Cade was going to do. He kissed her bare shoulders until he reached the delicate silk fabric where her bosom lay under. He pulled it gently until her beautiful full mounds danced in the moonlight. Cade delivered hot, melting kisses to them until her body quivered with desire. He sat her up and unzipped the dress and watched as the blue silk fabric lay at her feet. She removed his trousers and marveled in the part of him that was swollen with the need for her. Cade swept her off her feet and laid her down on the blanket gently. He kissed her feverishly until she begged for more. "Cade, please, baby, come inside of me!" She moaned. She stroked the black matted chest and looked into his passion-filled eyes as he drove his manhood deep into her secret place. "OH!" she yelled as the shaft hit bottom. She was driving him mad. Her boldness was the ultimate reward. He loved how she could blush and be so innocent and yet be a lioness to his needs. Cade grunted loudly at the pleasure he felt. His rock-hard buttocks delivered thrust after thrust that sent her body soaring with desire. As she found that wonderful feeling of ecstasy, she begged him to join her. Cade's body rocked violently as he plunged deep inside her one last time. He jerked as his seed spilled into an already full womb. "Oh, Cade, I love you!" she yelled as the last wave hit her. Cade held her tightly against him as he followed her to the heavens. Their lovemaking had been so intense that Cade had not seen the onlooker. Mario had hid behind some trees and watched as the white woman begged her husband to take her. He had been taken away by desire himself as he saw her beautiful body. Even as she was with child, she took his breath. When the couple had made love, Mario relieved himself, swearing to get revenge on the rich man that had fired him. Cade slipped a robe that he had had the attendants lay there in case they decided to take a moonlight swim. She watched as Cade adorned his robe as well, and together they made their way back to the main house. When Maria saw them coming and they did not appear to be wet, she smiled at the realization of what happened. She quickly went out the back entrance to retrieve their clothes that had been left there. She had gathered them all up and started back to the house when she heard something behind her. She quickly turned to see what was there but saw nothing.

CHAPTER 12

Rebecca had dressed comfortably in a sundress and was so excited to go into the city. She wanted to see for herself what the town was like. After all, they were going to be staying here a good bit of their time after the baby was born. She wondered how they accepted outsiders. The baby was unusually active today, and she could not help but laugh at the cartwheels it was making. She grabbed her bag and started down the stairs to have breakfast with Cade. She was glad that it was a light breakfast because she was a little bit queasy this morning. Cade stood as she reached the table and kissed her sweetly. Her beauty always stunned him and made him catch his breath. "You are beautiful this morning, baby," Cade said as he hugged her tight. Rebecca sat down and barely touched her food. Cade asked, "What is the matter, sweetheart, are you not feeling well this morning?" Rebecca wrinkled her nose and replied, "I am a little queasy this morning, but it should soon go away." "Are you sure you do not want to lie around here until I return?" Cade asked, allowing her to back out if she wanted to. "No, baby, I will be fine, and I am terribly excited to go into town." She grabbed her throat in a wave of nausea; she felt of the beautiful necklace that he had presented her the first magical night they had arrived. Cade ate slowly to allow her time to eat, in hopes that she would begin to feel better. When she got up and finished her juice; standing, looking at the ocean, Cade said, "Well, my love, let us begin our shopping journey." Rebecca was so excited. When the limo picked them up at the front door, Cade waited till Rebecca was inside and sat next to her. The trip to town was about a half-hour long, and Cade used this time to point out some of the historical places that they would visit on the next trip. When he decided to buy the villa, he did not realize that some of their time would be spent handling the money transaction. They arrived at the bank, and Cade escorted Rebecca inside. She was treated like royalty when they arrived and was made very comfortable as Cade signed some papers and watched as his lawyer filed all the necessary papers to prove ownership. The men shook hands, and Cade came out with a huge smile on his face. He reached for her and walked toward the limo. Rebecca saw one of the bike-driven carts as they passed by, and the man offered to take them wherever they needed to go. Cade agreed and threw his suit jacket in the limo and told the driver to head back to the villa. Cade helped her in and sat next to her. Rebecca was amazed at the many different shops and variety of items they had for sale. She was amazed at how the market area was so chaotic and how they begged you to buy something from them. They had reached a small fruit stand, and Rebecca wanted to admire their produce when Cade decided to run across the street to get them something cool to drink. He watched carefully as Rebecca conversed with man at the stand. He turned to pay for the drinks, and when he started back to the cart, he could not find Rebecca anywhere. He asked the driver of the cart where she had gone and even he had not seen the direction she left in. Cade dropped the drinks as he started to panic. He told the driver of the cart to get off and help him find her. He promised a reward if he did. He was beside himself with worry. He had never had any bad experiences in his many journeys here, but Rebecca was a beautiful woman whom they would consider very wealthy. He remembered the jewelry that he had given her, and he knew that she had it on this morning at breakfast. This would make her a huge target. How could he have been so stupid to allow her to wear it?

Rebecca had been talking with the older Mexican man about his produce when someone came up behind her pretending he was with her. He whispered to her that if she did not follow him, he would cut the baby from her where she stood. Rebecca was beside herself with fear. She thought if she went with him, he would let her live. He brought her down an alleyway nearby and smiled at her with evil eyes that she was sure were undressing her. He snatched the necklace from her and said, "What is the matter, senorita, are you not going to beg for it back? Your husband only gave it to you a couple of nights ago." Rebecca had gotten a good look at him, and when he said that, she knew who he was. "If this will make you turn and leave me, then I will gladly sacrifice the necklace for the life of my child," Rebecca said bravely. Mario laughed at her response and began to insult her. "What is the matter, Mrs. Matthews, are you not going to beg me to come inside of you as you did your husband last night on the beach?" Rebecca knew that he had to have been there watching to know that. She also wondered who else at the villa may have been involved. With one quick jerk, he pulled the cotton material from her breasts and began to maul them.

Rebecca tried to fight him, but it was to no avail. He spun her around and pushed her against the wall of the building. He was crushing her stomach as he pushed her with his body weight against the wall. She was trying to fight him, but every time she would move her arm to fight him away, he would push her harder into the wall. She was in pain from the force of it and was horrified that he may be harming the baby. She held herself away from the wall as much as she could and began to scream. He put his hand over her mouth, and she could feel his swollen private part as it threatened to enter her. She screamed as loud as she could. She was crying uncontrollably, she closed her eyes and began to pray for the life of her child. Cade was racing down the sidewalk when he heard her scream. He followed the sound, and his mind raced at the thought of what he would find. When he reached the alleyway and saw the waiter that he had fired about to enter her, he lost all self-control. He also saw that he was crushing her up against the wall. The flashing thought of his unborn child being squeezed to death made him forget that this man was even human. He pulled him off Rebecca and threw him to the ground. He beat him with his bare hands until he could not hold himself up any longer. He was so enraged that he never heard the policeman blowing his whistle. The driver of the cart saw Rebecca exposed and took his shirt off to cover her. Rebecca sobbed uncontrollably as she held her stomach. When Cade came out of his anger-filled rage, he saw the commotion around him. He saw the diver holding Rebecca and raced to her side. Cade held her and began to yell, "Rebecca, please tell me that you are all right. My god, did he hurt you?" Rebecca could not speak; she was in a state of shock. The policeman had called an ambulance, and in no time, she was on her way to the hospital. Cade rode beside her and whispered of his love for her as they raced to the hospital. Rebecca was rushed into a cubicle, and a doctor began his examination of her. Cade ran his blood-covered hands through his hair as he paced the hall outside where she was. The policeman from the scene had arrived and called him, "Senor Matthews!" Cade spun around thinking it was the doctor with news of Rebecca and the baby. "Yes!" Cade responded, realizing it was the police. "Mr. Matthews, we have Marion Gonzalez in custody. We recovered this from the alleyway and knew it was probably your wife's. Mr. Gonzalez, if he lives, will spend the rest of his life in prison, this I assure you." Cade retorted, "It was my intention for him not to!" The policeman continued, "The old man at the produce stand told us what he had seen, and the cart driver told us his story as well. I will get a statement from your wife as soon as she is able. I am sorry about this, Mr. Matthews. I will be in touch." It seemed like hours before the doctor came out. Cade met him in the hallway. "Mr. Matthews, she is going to be fine. We have examined her and the baby, and they both are fine. Your wife is still very upset. She had some bruising on her ribs and her stomach, but other than that, she is fine. We also ran semen tests on her, and there was only one sample taken. I know this is personal but, did you have intercourse with your wife in the past twenty-four hours?" Cade remembered the sweet love that they had made on the beach. He wished he could rewind time and never had allowed this to happen to her. "Yes, yes, we have," Cade said. The doctor continued, "Well, it is our conclusion that he had not yet entered her. I will notify the police that it was only robbery and attempted rape." *RAPE!* Cade shuddered at the thought; he remembered how upset Rebecca was over the attack with Ezekiel, he hoped that she had not been scared for life. You may go in to see her now, she is asking for you. Cade entered her room, and his heart rose to his throat at what he saw. One side of her face was scratched where she had been pressed so roughly against the wall. Her beautiful full red lips were busted from the force of the monstrous hands that covered them. Her eyes were swollen from her hysterical crying, and she had a saddened look in them that broke his heart. Cade walked to her slowly, he gently picked her up from the bed and held her close. He sobbed as he said, "Oh my god, Rebecca, this is all my fault. Can you ever forgive me for doing this to you?" Rebecca was still too upset to answer. She wanted Cade to hold her and kiss this all away. They sobbed together for hours, and Cade held her the entire time. The sun was beginning to set in the sky, and Rebecca had drifted off to sleep. When the hospital intercom startled her awake, she asked, "Is there any reason they are holding me here?" Cade wiped the tears from his eyes and replied, "I don't think so, baby, why do you ask?" "I want to go back to the villa. I do not want to sleep here tonight. Please, Cade, take me home!" Rebecca said as she wiped tears from her face. Cade called for the nurse and told her of their wishes. She returned a few minutes later with papers for Rebecca to sign. Cade called for the limousine to come get them. Rebecca wore a hospital gown as she was wheeled to the door of the limo. The drive back to the villa was an emotional one. Rebecca could not hold the information that she knew any longer. "Cade, he watched us make love last night. He mocked the way I talked to you when we did it. He had to have been there. He even told me where we where. He was planning this even then. He was angry because you fired him. I want you to ask Maria if anyone knew he was there. If they did, I want them all gone," she said furiously. Cade could not believe that Mario had been there last night. How could he have been that close and never been seen. When they pulled up to the house, Maria was waiting at the door. She was shocked to see Rebecca. The beautiful woman that left this morning was not the lady that was getting out of the car now. When Cade brought her inside, he carried her up the stairs. When he opened the door to their bedroom, he saw that Maria had drawn a warm bath. The air was filled with the smell of relaxing lavender. Cade asked, "Rebecca, baby, do you want this, or would you rather go straight to bed?" Rebecca remembered the warm relaxing bath and answered, "I will bath, I want to wash all of this off me." Cade knew what "all of this" she was referring to. If only he could rewind time and do this day over. His precious Rebecca would not have had to go through this. He sat her down, and Maria stepped in to remove her gown; she sat it down in a chair beside the tub and motioned for Cade to leave them. Maria had been with the property for years. She was a trusted friend; whatever she had in mind, he trusted her enough to know it was for their good. Cade sat outside the door as he listened to Maria. "Senorita, this was a bad thing that happened to you this day. I am terribly sorry for this." Rebecca smiled as she gently sank into the tub of warm water. "Do you consider me a friend, Mistress Matthews? Maria asked. "Yes, Maria, I have grown quite fond of you, why do you ask?" Rebecca responded. "Then I feel it is my duty as your friend to share something with you. When you arrived here only a few days ago, I was amazed by your beauty and your innocence. Senor Cade is a good man, and I was pleased that he had found such beauty but more so with a beautiful, innocent heart. The happiness that you found together is growing inside you even at this moment. This happiness that you have found is a rare and precious thing. This thing that was done to you today was done to you by a monster that witnessed this. He only saw your beauty and thought he could take it away from you. You must wash this from you now. When you leave this tub, you will put all of this behind you. If you chose not to, this will fester and grow, and it will eat the both of you until this monster has consumed you both. Let this child that grows inside you be born to a strong, wise, beautiful mother that will not let this monster win. I want you to close your eyes and visualize as I bath you that all that has happened to you today is being taken from you. I will take this gown and burn it in this fireplace when we are finished, and it will forever be forgotten," Maria said firmly as she took Rebecca's chin in her hand and kissed her forehead. Rebecca knew she was right. As Maria bathed her, she pictured in her mind that she had been cleansed from the scar that this monster had made. When Maria was through, she did as she said and burned the hospital gown. Rebecca stood still as she brushed her beautiful long hair. Rebecca released the towel from her and crawled into bed. Maria picked the towel up from the floor and left the room. Cade had listened to all that she had said to Rebecca. Cade grabbed Maria and thanked her for all that she had done. "Maria, Mario was here last night. He watched Rebecca and I while we were on the beach. He told her of our conversation. Did any of the attendants know that he was here or helped him in any way?" Maria thought about what she had heard. She told Cade of this and reassured him that the attendants that he had hired today were from her family. She told him that Mario was a friend of her son who needed money, and he had worked for several villa owners without complaints. Cade instructed her to not hire anyone unless they had been checked out by him from now on. "Thank you again, Maria, we are very fortunate to have you." Cade went inside the bedroom. Rebecca lay in the huge plush bed, resting as he walked in. "How are you, my love?" Cade asked, feeling very stupid for asking the question. Rebecca answered, "I am feeling much better. Maria is a kind woman." Cade shook his head in agreement as he said, "I am going to get a quick shower." Rebecca lay down and watched Cade undress, admiring his beautiful body. She was going to try to act as if this whole thing did not happen. That was the only thing that would work. None of this was either of their faults, and it would take time to completely be over it, but she was not going to let a monster tear apart the love that she and Cade had for one another. When Cade came to bed, Rebecca was lying in the candlelit room waiting for him. She kissed him sweetly as he entered their bed. Cade was surprised by her actions and said, "I love you, Rebecca! If there is anything you need, please, baby, let me know." Rebecca replied, "There is one thing that I need, my love." Cade quickly said, "Name it and it shall be done." "Make love to me, Cade, and wipe the memory of this day from my mind." Cade was shocked at her request and wondered if he should refuse because of her condition. He knew she needed to be held and comforted. He took her gently into his arms and made the sweetest love that he had ever made to her. He put his needs aside, and this was about Rebecca and what she needed. He simply thought about what he had and what could have been taken away in a blink of an eye. After hours of lovemaking, Cade held her close against him as she drifted to sleep. He lay there listening to her troubled breathing and knew that she was once again fighting the monster that threatened to consume her. He kissed her face and called her back to him; he made love to her all night long so sweetly and so tenderly that when they awoke the next morning, Rebecca could not help but awake with a smile on her face. The baby rolled and tumbled as if it were delighted the sun had come up. Rebecca had gotten up and pulled her thirsty robe over her and hurried downstairs to where Cade was waiting for her. He was on the veranda talking to the doctor that had attended to her in the emergency room. When Rebecca came through the French doors, the sight of the doctor stopped her in her tracks. "Good morning, sweetheart! You were sleeping so soundly when I woke up I decided to let you sleep as long as you wanted. Do you remember Dr. Sanchez?" "Yes, I do. Good morning," Rebecca said with a smile. Cade continued, "Dr. Sanchez came by to check on you this morning and to discuss a matter with both of us, baby." "Well, I know that yesterday was a terrible, unfortunate thing, and I feel that some good news can oftentimes help relieve some of this. Yesterday when we were running some tests, we did an ultrasound, and it revealed the sex of your baby. I thought it might bring happier times if you knew." Rebecca looked at Cade and smiled. "Cade, are you opposed to us finding out before it is actually born?" "Not at all, I would love to know!" He wrapped his arms around Rebecca's waist as Dr. Sanchez was about to reveal the sex of their baby. "Well, Rebecca and Cade, I am pleased to tell you that you are going to have a girl!" Rebecca could not contain the tears any longer. She put her hands over her mouth and then hugged Cade tightly. "Oh my god!" Cade said as pride radiated from him. "Oh, Rebecca, baby, a girl! That is the most wonderful news." Rebecca could not believe the news. She had not really thought about whether she wanted a girl or a boy. However, now that she knew, she would not have had it any other way. Maria came into the room with a fresh pot of decaffeinated coffee. She saw all the excitement on everyone's face and thought that to be unusual for such an occasion as this. Rebecca saw her bewilderment and said, "Maria, Dr. Sanchez came by to tell Cade and I that we are having a girl!" Maria started throwing her hands and saying something in Spanish that she could not understand. Maria hugged Rebecca gently and said, "I am so very happy for you, Senor and Senorita Matthews, that is very good news for you to hear today." Maria exclaimed. Dr. Sanchez drank a cup of coffee with them and then left. Rebecca could not wipe the smile from her face. She held her stomach lovingly, thinking of her daughter that lay there. Cade came up behind her and held her tightly. She tensed for a moment and then, overcoming the fear that was locked in her subconscious mind, fell into Cade's arms. "Well, baby, what shall we name our little girl?" Cade said as he kissed her cheek. He could kick himself for scaring her. He could never do that again. Rebecca thought about it for a moment and asked, "What about Destiny, because you are mine, and Grace because of the mercy that was shown to all of us yesterday." Cade said,

"Destiny Grace Matthews, I love it!" He dropped to his knees and pulled apart the robe that covered her belly. He kissed it lovingly and said, "Good morning, Destiny Grace, I cannot wait to hold you." At that moment, she kicked at the spot that Cade had just seconds ago kissed. Cade and Rebecca laughed loudly.

CHAPTER 13

They left the villa, and Rebecca had mixed emotions about leaving. She was excited to go to her new home and prepare Destiny's nursery. But a part of her did not want to leave the beautiful Spanish villa. Despite the attack, she loved her getaway place and looked forward to bringing her daughter here. Although it was enormous, it had a homey feel that delighted her.

Cade held her hand as they boarded the plane. Rebecca was surprised as they entered the plane that Joana and Kirby had been replaced with older, more mature attendants. Cade never mentioned it, but Rebecca was grateful that he was that thoughtful to her insecurities. She went to the restroom, and then she seated herself in the chair and fastened her seat belt. Cade spoke to Michael and took his coat off and sat next to her. As the plane started taxiing down the runway, Cade grabbed her hand and kissed it gently. When they had reached cruising altitude, Rebecca removed her seat belt and once again watched the clouds billow by the wings of the plane. Destiny suddenly decided to kick forcefully, and when Rebecca let out a noise, Cade was at her side in an instant. "Rebecca, are you all right, baby?" She responded by taking his hand and placing it near the spot that she had just kicked. When she delivered another kick, Cade was amazed at the intensity. Rebecca continued to watch the clouds as they turned to gray. When she saw the lightning bolt, she jumped once again. Cade reached for her hand and carried her over to the couch. He held her, comforting her, and explained that it was only a thunderstorm and they would make it through it shortly. Rebecca felt better as Cade rubbed her stomach and kissed her full red lips that had finally healed from the brutal attack. The oldest of the new attendants came with a tray of refreshments and said, "Hello, Mr. and Mrs. Matthews, my name is Linda. I hope that you will find everything to your liking, and we can make you as comfortable as possible while you travel home. I trust that your trip to Cozumel was a good one. Rebecca smiled and quickly answered,

"Yes, we found out that we are having a little girl there!" Cade was surprised at her answer, after what had happened to her there, he was sure that the trip had been ruined. After all, it was all he could do to keep the memory of her pressed up against the wall with Mario holding his member trying to enter her out of his mind. He was tormented by it often. He wasn't sure how Rebecca was able to remove it from her mind so easily. He had heard all that Maria had said; however, it was his fault that this happened to his precious Rebecca, and the guilt was killing him. Linda smiled and commented, "Oh, congratulations, I know that has got to be exciting for you!" Rebecca sat, smiling out the window. She was excited to go see her beautiful farmhouse with everything they had bought for it. It was going to be lovely, and she hoped that it had the same coziness that she had felt at the villa. When the plane set down, Rebecca could see Cade's car sitting nearby. Linda opened the door, and Cade said his goodbyes to Michael. They watched as their luggage was loaded into his car. They hardly spoke anything to each other on the way to the house, but Rebecca decided that Cade just had a lot on his mind. "Cade, are you all right? You have been really quiet today, baby," Rebecca asked as she rubbed his shoulder. Cade was not going to lie to her, but he did not want to bring up the subject of the attack. "I am nervous about seeing the house, I guess, and a bit tired from the trip. I do have something else on my mind, but I would really like to tell you about it later," Cade said as he smiled at her lovingly. Rebecca knew by the smile that he was not upset with her over anything, and she would be happy with that for now. When they started up the drive to the house, Rebecca giggled like a child. They had even decorated the porch with plants and greenery. "Oh, Cade, it is beautiful!" she said breathlessly. Cade stopped the car and opened her door. He held her hand as they started up the steps to her porch. Rebecca was about to open the front door when Cade swept her off her feet. "I am supposed to carry my bride over the threshold, aren't I?" Rebecca laughed at the thought. When they opened the door, Rebecca was speechless. The house was so lovely that she was stunned. The furniture that they had picked for the living room was perfect. It allowed for comfort and coziness but also was really beautiful in the room. They walked and looked at each room. Cade was really pleased with how it looked as well. When they opened the door to the master suite, Rebecca giggled with delight. Cade had insisted on purchasing another bedroom suite, declaring that the one in the apartment was far too masculine for them to use in a bedroom for them both. The one they chose had a canopy with beautiful fabric streaming from it. She turned to look at the room that Cade had remodeled that led from their room to an adequate-size nursery. It was precious, and she knew that Destiny was going to love it. The bright yellow was the perfect color. Rebecca hugged Cade tightly and said, "Cade, I love it! It is perfect! We are going to be so happy here." Cade wanted to be so desperately; he wanted to let go of this guilt that he carried, but he was not sure how. They returned to the kitchen, and Rebecca marveled at the sight. She was going to love cooking in here. She could not wait to fill the air with the smell of bread and cakes. She wondered if Destiny would love to bake as well. She made her way to the back porch and sat in her swing. She was at home here, and she could not wait till she could hear the sound of laughter in the yard as she sat in the swing. Cade came out and saw that she was lost in thought. He wondered if she was reliving that horrible day. He had to get this off his chest; his heart could not take another minute. He walked to her and kneeled in front of her. When he looked into her eyes, Rebecca was terrified at what she saw. Cade's eyes were filled with tears. "Cade? Baby, what is wrong?" she asked in a voice that conveyed her emotion. "Rebecca, the guilt of what happened to you is killing me. You will never be the same, and it is all my fault. You trusted me to take care of you, and I let you down. I should have never allowed you to be by yourself, and I should have made you take the necklace off before we left. I am so sorry, baby! I cannot get the image of you pressed up against the wall fighting for your life and the life of our child. You're half-naked body with his hands on you . . . GODDAMIT!" Cade yelled as he stood up and ran his fingers through his black hair. He paced back and forth in front of her with tears falling down his face. Rebecca was both shocked and mortified that he had been carrying this guilt this whole time. Was he upset because he felt as if this was his fault, or was it because another man put his hands on her in that way? She thought back to when she told him about Ezekiel. She had to help relieve himself from this guilt. She stood in front of him with tears in her eyes and said, "Cade, baby, I do not blame you at all for what happened to me. You fired him because you saw something in him that made you uncomfortable. You did that to protect me. You had no way of knowing what he was capable of. I am quite sure that if I had not been wearing the necklace, he would have done the same thing. You cannot hold yourself responsible for this. You have done all you could do. My god, you saved me from him in the end, he might even be dead by now! This baby and I are alive today because *you* saved us, what more could I ask of you!" Cade looked into her eyes and was unable to speak. She held him rubbing his hair, kissing him softly. Cade looked into her eyes and said, "I love you! If I would have lost you—"

Rebecca put her finger over his lips and said, "But you didn't, you saved me. You have got to let this guilt go, Cade, or it will tear you, and eventually us, apart." She took his hand and pressed it to her stomach. Destiny was vigorously kicking. She looked deep into his eyes and said, "She and I are depending on you. We have something so special, Cade. You are what I have dreamed about all my life. Let it go." Cade kissed her lips tenderly; he rubbed her stomach while holding her close to him. When their lips parted, she continued, "I do not want anyone to know what happened, and unless you need to, I would like for us to never discuss this again. It is forgotten." Cade shook his head in agreement and lifted her off her feet. He carried up the stairs to their bedroom where he made tender, sweet love to her. They enjoyed each other for the rest of the afternoon.

They were lying in each other's arms when the doorbell rang. Cade quickly got up and grabbed his robe. He rushed to see who it was. Rebecca got up and did the same. She had made it halfway down the stairs when he heard Gloria's voice. Gloria said, "Oh god, Cade, did I interrupt something?" When she saw Rebecca wearing a robe too, she quickly said, "I can come back later." And she began to walk toward the door. "Mother, it is okay. We are finished, please come back in." "I am sorry to interrupt. I started to wait till in the morning, but I decided to cook dinner for all of us. I have it in the car. Cade, will you come help?" Cade smiled at Rebecca because he knew that his mother was a little uncomfortable. Rebecca put her hand over her mouth at the face he was making. "Yes, Mother, I would be glad to," Cade said as he followed his mother out the door. Rebecca went to her new kitchen and started setting the table. When Cade brought the food in and sat it down, the aroma filled the house. Rebecca was reminded that she had not eaten since breakfast, and she was famished. Gloria began to plate the wonderful-smelling food as Cade poured wine for him and his mother. They sat and ate, and Cade told his mother all about the villa. "Mother, Rebecca and I were going to call you in the morning anyway. We have some really wonderful news to tell you." Rebecca smiled at Cade because she knew what he was talking about. "While we were in Mexico, we found out the sex of the baby. Rebecca and I are pleased to tell you that you are getting a granddaughter! We have decided to name her Destiny Grace." Gloria screamed for joy. She found it very hard to contain her joy. They discussed the subject for a while, and Gloria asked, "Why did you have an ultrasound done down there, Rebecca, was there some problem?" Cade sat his glass down and gave Rebecca a worried look. He had not realized that his mother would pick up on it. Rebecca saw the quandary that Cade was in and spoke up, "Gloria, I had a little mishap while I was shopping, and they thought it best that I go to the hospital to get checked out. There is nothing wrong." Gloria could tell by the look on her son's face that she was telling the whole truth. She also realized that she did not want to talk about it. Gloria replied, "Oh, I am so glad, dear." When they finished, Rebecca cleared the table and excused herself. She went upstairs to relieve herself. While she was upstairs, Gloria thought it would be a great time to look at the rest of the house. Cade quickly showed her the downstairs and was very anxious to show her the nursery. Rebecca was not expecting anyone to be up there, and when she accidently bumped into Gloria, she screamed as if someone was attacking her. Cade grabbed her and immediately started shouting, "Rebecca, it's okay, baby, it is Mother!" He held her close, stroking her head and back. Rebecca was crying uncontrollably. When Cade had calmed her down, they both looked at Gloria who was also crying. Rebecca felt very bad for her and said, "Gloria, I am so sorry! I did not mean to react that way." Cade could see that she was terribly embarrassed by the whole thing and said, "Bec, we need to tell her." Rebecca shook her head in agreement and said, "Okay, but can we go back downstairs and sit? I think I am going to have a sip of wine." Cade held her hand as the threesome went back into the kitchen. Rebecca took Cade's glass and took a huge sip of his wine. Cade cleared his throat and began, "Mother, the first night we were at the villa, I noticed one of the attendants was paying too much attention to Rebecca. It was obvious that he found her very attractive, and being the jealous man that I am, I dismissed him. I thought I was being more than generous when I gave him a whole week's pay. Before I fired him that night, at dinner, I gave Rebecca a necklace, and he saw the whole thing. When he heard the news, he was angry, only I did not know this because I let Maria fire him. She is after all the one to do that. It was a couple of days later when I decided to buy the villa, when I needed to go into town, I gave Rebecca the choice to go with me and to see the sights. We were looking around at the shops when I decided to get us something to drink. Rebecca was talking to a man about some produce, and I was watching her the whole time. When I turned away for a moment to pay for our drink and turned back, Rebecca was nowhere to be found. I began searching immediately and remembered that she had the necklace on when we left. When I found her, the waiter had her in an alleyway. He had her pressed up against the wall and was crushing her. He had torn her clothes off and was about to . . ." Cade looked at Rebecca and saw the tears streaming down her face. He went over and held her close to her. Gloria had turned away from them and had put her hands over her mouth. She was stunned at what she had heard. Rebecca turned and, with a broken voice, picked up where Cade had stopped. "He pulled him off me and beat that man nearly to death. If it had not been for him, Destiny and I very easily could be dead right now." Cade and Rebecca watched as Gloria's shoulders jerked. They knew she was beside herself with sympathy. Cade took Rebecca by the hand and went over embracing her. Cade held the two women as they all three cried. When Gloria finally calmed herself, she said, "Rebecca, words cannot tell you how very sorry I am, dear. If I had known, I would have been so careful not to startle you. I am so thrilled that Cade stopped that monster! I also am very proud of you for dealing with it as you had. You must put this behind you, or it will tear the precious love that you have for one another apart." Rebecca wiped her eyes and said, "I know. Cade and I had put it aside, and I had asked that we tell no one about it. I do not want to talk about it ever again. I especially do not want my parents to find out about it. The aftereffects will get easier to live with, and I will not react that way forever. Please know that I am sorry that I reacted that way. It was not your fault and do not blame yourself at all." Gloria walked away wiping her eyes. She took a long sip of her wine and changed the subject. "May we go look at where my precious little granddaughter is going to be sleeping soon? I came in as the movers got here, but I was not able to see the room finished." They all walked upstairs. Gloria loved the room and went on and on about going clothes shopping. "We have to get something for her to come home to from the hospital, you know." Rebecca looked at Cade for approval and said, "Gloria, I asked Cade if I could deliver at home. I will continue to see Dr. Goldstein until time, but if everything is going good, I want to have Destiny here. I would love it if you were here as well to share this experience with us." Gloria was a little shocked at the idea but realized that Amish women gave birth at home quite often. "I am going to find a midwife who will deliver her. We won't be without medical help, and the hospital is not that far away. I feel really good about it. The whole experience is not new to me. I have been with my mother for several of my siblings' births, and it is so much less stressful and, believe it or not, much less painful." Gloria saw that Rebecca was not blind to all that came with a birthing process and said, "I think that if that's what you would like to do, I would be honored to be here to see her come into the world." The threesome returned downstairs, and Rebecca and Cade cleaned the dishes as Gloria sat nearby and chatted. It was almost midnight when she decided to leave. They said their good nights and stood and watched as she drove away. Cade and Rebecca returned inside the house in silence. He set the burglar alarm as

Rebecca turned most of the lights out, and they retired to their bedroom. Rebecca took off her robe and climbed into bed, and Cade was right behind her. He loved how she felt next to him. They talked about finding a midwife as they fell asleep.

The next couple of days went by rather fast as Rebecca did the final touches on their new house. It had been a couple of weeks since she had visited her parents, and she wanted to ask Cade if they could go by there tomorrow after her doctor visit. She walked through the house in search of him when she discovered he was in the study. The door was open, and she walked in. Cade was in the process of setting up his computer when he saw her come in. "Hello, gorgeous, how did you know that I was missing you?" he said mischievously. Rebecca loved that tone he talked to her when he was thinking about her in naughty ways. She came around to his chair and pushed the papers that were hampering her from sitting on his desk. When she was seated, she said, "Because I was missing you too, my love!" Cade eyed the knee-length dress as it gave hints of what was just out of sight. Rebecca put her hands on his shoulders; one of the small straps that kept the dress in place fell down her arm, giving little concealment to the full breast that lay underneath. Cade's body suddenly went hot with desire. Rebecca could see that he wanted her, and she decided she would tease him further. She pulled the dress up and spread her legs to reveal the treasure that it once hid. She also removed the other strap that cried for relief. Cade moaned roughly and began kissing the top of her beautiful bosom. Rebecca threw her head back in delight and pulled him closer to her. Cade picked her up and swept everything off his desk. He laid her down gently and removed his pants and shirt. When her naked body touched his, she tingled at the heat of it. He positioned her so that her buttocks rested at the end of the table. He gently slid the delicate panties from her perfect hips and tossed them to the ground. When he lowered himself between her legs, Rebecca ran her fingers through his long black hair. She pulled him deep into her and quivered in delight as he licked her womanly place. Rebecca moved her hips, mimicking the motion that he would make as he plunged his manhood deep inside her. She fought to savor the wonderful feeling as he delighted her with his tongue. When Rebecca could not keep the flames from getting any higher, she gave in and welcomed the wonderful feeling of ecstasy as it consumed her. Cade knew when her body went suddenly limp that she had returned from the clouds. He kissed the path that led over their child and to her voluptuous breast. He saw her flushed red cheeks that told of her climax. He wrapped her legs around him and sat her down on the floor.

Cade sat down in his chair and pulled her over his throbbing member. He wrapped his fingers in her long ringlets while he plunged himself deep into her treasure. She whimpered as it brought her great pleasure. Cade yelled, "Rebecca, my baby, I love you!" He lifted her once more and once again laid her on the table. When he entered her this time, he had done so with the tenderness that matched his love for her. He pulled her hands above her head and wrapped his fingers around hers. He kissed her over and over. He felt her beautiful body, finally ending up at her stomach. He caressed it gently as he looked passionately into Rebecca's eyes. He put one hand underneath her buttock, and the other caressed her face gently. He stared at her face as if he were trying to memorize every inch of her face. Rebecca's lips parted in satisfaction, and Cade quickly captured them and searched them with his tongue. Rebecca could taste her juices as his tongue dove deeper and deeper. Her body was on fire. When Cade's rhythm grew faster, she could not help but yell with pleasure, "Oh, baby, I—" Cade felt her body jerk as her release came. He felt the gentle kisses that her womanly place gave him in gratitude of the relief. The pleasure was so intense that Cade allowed his body the release it cried out for. His body shook violently as a force of the explosion. Cade kissed her tenderly and said, "Rebecca, my heart is so full of love for you. I fear sometimes that I am going to melt. You have captured me in such a way that I do not want to be free." Rebecca looked deeply into his eyes and replied, "My love for you is so powerful and so strong that I fear that I would not live without it." He lay beside her enjoying her body. Even now as they lay there together, he did not want to leave her side. They felt Destiny play inside Rebecca's stomach as he was caressing her abdomen, and Cade realized that the hard desk was probably not comfortable for her. He crawled off and gently lifted her to stand. Cade grabbed their clothes, and they walked naked up the stairs. Cade started the shower, and Rebecca crawled in with him. She enjoyed bathing him, and he watched as her soft touch and the warm suds brought his body to life once more. He pressed her against the wall, and suddenly the images of Mario and that day flashed before his eyes. He quickly released her, picking her gently and wrapping her legs around him. He took her again, and soon the love that he felt for her drove the demon from his mind. As the warm, soapy water washed over them, they gave in to their release. Cade pressed his hand against the wall to steady himself as his release shook his innermost being. Rebecca moaned softly as she felt his seed once more release inside her. She clung tightly to him and once more climbed to the heavens.

CHAPTER 14

The weeks passed by quickly, and Rebecca and Cade were anxiously waiting the arrival of their daughter. Dr. Goldstein had agreed to a home delivery and recommended a woman for them. Rebecca and Cade had gone to meet her, and the instant they shook hands, Rebecca felt at ease. They had made all their last-minute plans and felt really confident that they would work. Cade had insisted that Rebecca not be left alone and had rallied the help of his mother when on the rare occasion that he would have to be away for any reason. Rebecca had gotten up and started her day as any other and, aside from the usual aches and pains, felt no different. She was on the back porch sipping her coffee, waiting for Cade to end a phone call with a business associate when a sudden pain struck her. She felt warm liquid as it wet the bottom of her thirsty robe and knew immediately what had happened. She stood up and held her stomach tightly as the pain subsided. When Cade turned around and saw her and the blood all over her robe, he froze. "Rebecca!" he yelled as he hung up the phone. Rebecca looked up and smiled. "Today is the day that Destiny has decided to be born," she said calmly. Cade rushed over to her and helped her to sit. "You know what to do, baby, just stay calm. I need you to help me to the shower, and then you may call Isabelle and your mother," Rebecca stated calmly. In his panicked state, Cade picked her up and carried her to the stairs. Rebecca could not help but smile at his antics, but she never said a word. When he had arrived at the shower, he sat her down gently. He was about to walk away when another pain hit her. Rebecca grabbed his shoulder and held it tightly. She took long deep breaths, and in a few moments, it was gone. Cade grabbed her and hugged her to him. He tenderly kissed her lips and said, "Baby, are you sure about this?" Rebecca replied, "Very sure, I want Destiny to be born in her home with her family here, not some cold hospital by their rules. This is going to be fine, baby, just trust me." She took her robe off and started in the shower. Cade could not believe he had not noticed how much her stomach had fallen in the past few days. He marveled at her very pregnant body. He thought she was the most beautiful woman that he had ever seen. Even now when she was actually in labor, he could not help how his body reacted to her. He forced himself to pull the phone from his pocket. He called Isabelle and then his mother. He helped Rebecca dry off and got her a clean robe. Rebecca stood at the mirror, brushing her long wet hair. Her robe was open down the front, and Cade admired her beauty from afar. He walked to her and pulled her to his chest. He kissed her neck and ran his hand lovingly over her stomach; he nuzzled her ear and whispered, "I love you, sweetheart. I am so excited. I also must confess that I am a little scared." Rebecca turned to look him in the eyes and said, "I love you, Cade, very much. I am a little scared myself." Another pain hit her, and she began to breathe laboriously once again. Isabelle arrived first, and Cade rushed downstairs to greet her. "She is upstairs, and her contractions are about ten minutes apart." He and Isabella rushed upstairs and found Rebecca resting in a wooden rocking chair in the nursery. "How are you holding up, dear?" Isabella asked as she laid her supplies on the floor. She began to get her things that she needed out of the bag. When she reached for her blood pressure cuff and started taking vital signs, Rebecca answered, "I think I am fine, but you tell me." Isabella laughed and replied, "Everything is great!" When the doorbell rang again, Cade knew that it was his mother; he again rushed downstairs and let her in. Gloria hugged him tightly and said, singing, "I am going to be a grandmother today!" Cade laughed and motioned for her to go upstairs. Cade introduced the ladies and sat at Rebecca's side. A couple of hours had passed, and Rebecca's body was being assaulted by contractions. Isabella had darkened the room and lit some aromatic candles to help relax her. Rebecca had walked to the bed and lay down to rest, and Cade went to lay beside her. He was gently massaging her back when the next pain hit. Rebecca stood and began to try to position herself to ease the pain. She bit her lip at the intensity of it, and Isabella decided that she would check her after this one was gone. When the pain had subsided and Rebecca had begun to breathe easier, Isabella told her what she was going to do. Rebecca sat on the edge of the bed, pulled one leg up. Isabella adorned a pair of gloves and was amazed to find that she had already dilated seven centimeters. Rebecca smiled at the progress, but she also knew the worst was yet to come. Cade watched as Rebecca's body was racked with pain over and over. His heart was breaking at the sight of her agony. He also gained a whole new respect for her because of what she was doing. She wanted

Destiny to be born in her own home surrounded by her family. His heart filled with so much love for her his eyes began to fill with tears. He could not take it any longer; he had to hold her in his arms. He grabbed her just as the next wave hit. Rebecca tried to show no emotion, but Cade could tell that she was livid with pain. He wanted desperately to take this pain from her. Gloria watched as the two gained strength from one another. She also saw the struggle that Cade was having watching Rebecca endure the pain. Another hour passed, and Rebecca had begun to feel a great amount of pressure. Isabella laid out waterproof sheets on the bed and began to lay her sterile supplies out. Gloria was helping as Cade helped support Rebecca as she paced. When Rebecca let out a whimper, Cade knew this was different. He lifted Rebecca and carried her to the bed. Isabella waited till the pain had left and once again checked her for progress. "You are complete, my dear! We are fixing to have a baby," Isabella said softly. Cade kissed Rebecca tenderly. Rebecca positioned herself on the edge of the bed as she had seen her mother do many times. She told Cade to sit in front of her on the floor. Isabella stood nearby, but Rebecca had already told her that unless there was something wrong, she wanted Cade to take the baby from her. Rebecca pulled the robe off and laid it on the floor under her. When the next pain struck her, she began to gently bear it down. Rebecca felt the head as it made its way to the outside world. She motioned for Cade to hold her hands. She took his hands, and together they lifted Destiny into the world. Cade was crying uncontrollably as he lifted his daughter unto her mother's stomach. He kissed Rebecca's lips over and over as he watched his daughter take her first breath. Isabella came to make sure that she was all right, and when Destiny let out her first cry, they all began to clap joyously. Rebecca held her healthy infant to her and cried tears of joy. Cade came around to sit behind them and watched his beautiful wife hold their daughter. Isabella cut the cord and finished delivering the afterbirth. Rebecca lifted her daughter to her breast, and they all watched her hungrily suckle. Cade had never seen such a beautiful sight as this. He was overcome with emotion and cried uncontrollably. He held tightly to the two things that he loved and needed the most. "Oh my god, Rebecca, you are so amazing, my love!" he said as he kissed her lips over and over. Gloria watched and cried with him. Cade could not take his eyes off Rebecca and Destiny. Gloria and Isabella knew that the new family needed to be by themselves and went downstairs. Cade sat with Rebecca pulled tightly to his chest. They held their daughter and could not believe the awesomeness of what just happened. Cade stroked Rebecca's hair and said, "I hated watching the pain you were going through. I felt so helpless and useless. I have never been around this before, so I did not know what to expect, but I now know why you did this, and I must say that this was the most beautiful thing that I have ever been a part of. Thank you for this and thank you for enduring this. My heart is going to surely burst with the amount of love that I feel for you right now. I would have never believed that I could love you any more. I can also see why your father and mother had so many. This is the most wonderful thing there is compared to anything else. I want to fill this house with children." Rebecca laughed with tears streaming down her face. She hugged him and said, "Would you like to get started now?" Cade kissed her hungrily and answered, "Whenever you like!"

The couple lay there for hours. Isabella came in to check on Rebecca and to bring her food. Gloria sat and watched her son and was amazed at how he looked so comfortable with her already. Isabella took the infant from him to give her, her first bath. Cade watched carefully how it was done. Isabella weighed her and took her measurements and quickly diapered and clothed her. She handed the crying infant back to Cade and laughed loudly when she immediately hushed. "She already knows who her father is, doesn't she, Mommy?" Isabella said sweetly. Cade loved how that sounded and looked at Rebecca lovingly. She smiled at him, understanding what he was conveying. She watched as her beautiful husband pranced with their daughter in his arms. It was not too long before she drifted off to sleep. When she woke up, Cade had brought the rocker from the nursery and had it beside their bed rocking their precious daughter. Cade came to sit on the edge of the dimly lit room and kissed Rebecca's lips. "I think our daughter is hungry, my love." Rebecca sat up and let out one breast from her robe. Cade watched in amazement as Destiny nursed hungrily. He kissed Rebecca on her naked shoulder and said, "I have seen many sides of your beauty, and I think this puts all the others to shame." Rebecca kissed him tenderly. When Destiny was finished, Cade laid her in her bassinet that had been placed at their bedside. He crawled beneath the covers and held Rebecca in his arms. He loved this woman, and he loved his life. He wanted to show her how much. When Rebecca awoke the next morning, her room was filled with pink roses and balloons. The sight of all of them made her lose her breath; Cade came in the door with a bundle of pink balloons and a small box that had been wrapped to perfection. "Cade, they all are beautiful!" Gloria came in with Destiny in her arms. Cade said, "Our daughter wants her breakfast, but first, I want her mommy to open something." He sat down on the bed at Rebecca's side and handed her the box. Gloria came and sat on the other side and was beaming with excitement. Rebecca began to tear at the bow and paper. When she finally opened the box, her eyes filled with tears. Gloria gasped at the sight of it as well. Rebecca marveled at the matching pink diamond pendants—one for her and a tiny version for Destiny. Cade removed Rebecca's and placed it on her neck. Rebecca wiped the tears that were streaming down her face. "I had these made shortly after we found out that we were having Destiny. I will have one made for every daughter we have," Cade said as he kissed her lips lovingly. Gloria handed her swaddled infant to her, and Rebecca smiled when Destiny turned to look at her. Cade took the tiny necklace from the box and laid it on her chest. "She looks lovely with her very first piece of jewelry on," Gloria said as she laughed. Rebecca smiled up at Cade and said, "Yes, she does, but I am positive that will not be her last."

CHAPTER 15

They had settled into parenthood with grace, and Rebecca was reminded daily about how lucky she was. She loved to watch Cade with his daughter and thought it to be one of her favorite times. The weather had turned cold, and Thanksgiving was next week. She wondered if her parents would consider coming to her house for a celebration. She wondered if Cade would agree. Cade had just come into the room from putting Destiny's car seat in his car. "Cade, what do you think about having Thanksgiving dinner for my family and yours here if my parents will agree to it. I suppose that Kelly's parents should be invited too. I know if I were a grandparent, I would want to spend as much time as I could with my grandbabies as I hope I will be able to one day." She smiled. "I think that is a terrific idea, baby. Are you sure you want to tackle a dinner like that so soon?" Cade said as he watched her brush her beautiful long hair. She stood in front of the mirror with her robe on. It had come untied, and her bare skin was barely showing. Cade could not take it any longer, he had to touch her. It had been two weeks since they had made love, and his need for her was building up. He kissed her neck and pulled one side of the robe open to reveal what lay underneath. He put his hand on her stomach and began to massage it lovingly. Her naked breast danced as he rubbed her flat stomach. Cade whispered in her ear, "You are so beautiful, Bec. I cannot wait to make love to you again." He turned her around and slid his hand into the open robe and filled each hand with her soft cheeks as he pulled her close to him. His hard, matted chest felt the fullness of her milk-filled breast, and it drove him mad. He let out a long sigh and claimed her lips passionately. He knew it was too soon to make love to her, but it had been too long since he had touched her intimately. He wanted her to know that he needed her desperately. Rebecca held him tightly to her. She loved the way he felt against her and longed for him to make love to her. She had only a short time to wait, but another minute would be too long. She moaned as she felt his shaft swollen with the need for her. Cade kissed her sweetly. "I do not want to, but I can wait till it is safe for you, baby. Our first time will be wonderful. I just could not stand not to touch your beautiful body, Rebecca," Cade said with a lust-filled voice. He set her back enough that he could close her robe as he made a face at having to do that. Rebecca smiled and tried herself to regain her composure. "Now back to the subject of Thanksgiving. I think having it here is a great idea, my only concern is that it may be too much for you and too soon. I can hire a chef to come prepare one if you would like that," Cade explained. Rebecca thought his concern was precious. "Cade, I feel great, and I am sure that Mother and Gloria will help me. Maybe Mother and the girls could come spend the night with us, and we could visit and do our baking at the same time," Rebecca said excitingly. Cade loved to see her enthusiasm. He was excited as well; he wanted their first holidays together to be very special. "I will call Mother and see if she will come help you as well. She could do the decorating for you. We want Destiny's first Thanksgiving to be very special. I also have a surprise for you, my love!" Rebecca turned and smiled. "I have a photographer coming here in the morning to take some pictures of my beautiful girls. I know you are not used to this, but it is something I think you will enjoy. Also, we need to have memories of her early weeks as well." Rebecca was terribly excited she said, "I love the idea, thank you for thinking of it, but I want you to be in some of the pictures too. I would like a huge family picture for our living room wall in fact." Cade smiled and quickly said, "Yes, that is a wonderful idea. I will commission an oil painting of it for the villa as well."

Rebecca finished dressing, and they took their new daughter on her very first car trip. When they arrived, Samuel and Mary were just finishing eating their lunch. Annie heard their car first and came running out the front door. She was so glad to see Rebecca. She came running and gave her a huge hug. Mary was down the steps and was at Rebecca's side in no time. When Rebecca turned, Cade already had Destiny out of her seat and was walking toward her. Mary put her hands at her heart, and her eyes started filling with tears. She held her hands out and said, "May I hold my first granddaughter?" Cade handed the tiny bundle to her and watched as she admired her. Samuel watched over Mary's shoulders, and he too became caught up in the emotion. Rebecca hugged her father gently as he kissed her forehead. Mary led the crowd into the house and sat in the wooden rocker that she had rocked all of her little ones in. Mary unwrapped the precious infant and inspected her fully. "Becca, she is beautiful! She has both of your looks," Mary said as she wrapped her back up and held her close to her. Rebecca smiled and said, "Yes, she has her father's black hair and nose." Cade quickly butted in and said, "Yes, and her mother's beautiful lips and sweet personality." Mary smiled at both of them and nodded in agreement. All of Rebecca's siblings one by one came by to inspect their new niece. When the parade was over, Destiny began to squirm. Rebecca looked at her mother and said, "It is time to feed her, may we go to your bedroom and sit?" Samuel quickly answered, "Cade and I will walk out to the barn and give you the privacy you need, dear." When the men had left, Rebecca took her daughter and began nursing her. Mary watched in wonder. She was so proud that her daughter was now holding her own little one. She knew that Rebecca had always wanted children. Mary also knew that she was going to be a wonderful mother. "My word, Rebecca, I am so thrilled that you now are holding her in your arms," Mary said sweetly. "Was her birth an easy one?" Rebecca rubbed the thick black hair on her head and began, "We had her at home with a midwife. I was in a great deal of pain of course, but altogether, I think it went really well. When she was born, Cade delivered her, and that was the most special part. Cade is a wonderful father, and he can't wait to have more," Rebecca said as laughed softly. Mary put her hands to her face and giggled with her. The ladies chatted about all that had been done. Rebecca told her of their trip to Mexico and about Cade buying her the villa. She also told her about their new house and started asking her about Thanksgiving when the men returned. Rebecca asked if the elders and Bishop Miller had made their decision about shunning and was delighted to hear that Rebecca could visit anytime. Rebecca told her father of their plans for Thanksgiving, and Samuel agreed to attend. Cade was the first to speak, "If it all right to do so, you all are welcome to come the night before and stay. I will hire a van to come get you all. If John and Kelly can come, I will have them picked up as well. Rebecca thought it would be a good idea that we invite Kelly's mother and father to come. She was concerned that they would be alone for Thanksgiving, being that Kelly is an only child. She also did not want them to miss Joseph and Jonathan's first Thanksgiving. This is a very special Thanksgiving for all of your grandchildren," Cade said, smiling at Rebecca. "I think that is a wonderful idea, Cade! We shall love to come for a visit," Samuel answered. Annie, Katie, and Sarah jumped for joy! They were so excited about their trip. "I will contact Kelly's parents and extend to them the same invitation. Cade's mother is coming as well, and there is plenty of room for all of you," Rebecca said as she could barely hold her excitement. "I will send the van for you on Wednesday morning about ten then!" Cade said. Samuel agreed. The crowd discussed their menu and visited for several hours. When Cade decided that it was time for them to go, the whole family walked them out and watched as Rebecca put Destiny in her car seat. Rebecca hugged everyone goodbye and sat in the backseat with Destiny. Rebecca talked the whole way back home. Cade was pleased to see her excitement. He was looking forward to this himself. He was thrilled to be a part of a big family and knew that this was going to be a very special Thanksgiving indeed. Rebecca began to name off all the things that she needed to do before her family arrived. Cade interrupted her and said, "Bec, I want to spend the day tomorrow finding us a full-time housekeeper. The house is too much for you to deal with on your own, and this will allow you more time with Destiny and I. I will call the maid service tomorrow and set up some interviews." Rebecca thought about it and asked, "I wished we could find someone like Maria!" Cade knew that Maria had made a huge impression on Rebecca, and he did owe a debt of gratitude for bringing Rebecca out of the dark time after her attack. He would call a friend in the Mexican government first thing in the morning and see if that could be done. He would have to call Maria first thing to make sure that she would even want to. Cade went to sleep thinking of how he was going to pull this surprise off.

When the photographer came, Rebecca was so excited to see her. She set up her equipment and began giving Rebecca ideas for their photographs. She listened intently to them all and settled on a few. They spent several hours taking pictures. This allowed Cade time to make some calls, and much to his surprise, it went much easier than he had anticipated. Maria was delighted at the idea and was very excited to come to the states. Rebecca spent the next few days making calls and getting all of her plans for Thanksgiving made. She had called the grocer and gave them her list over the phone, and Cade's mother ran errands and planned the decorations. Rebecca had forgotten to ask if he had any success in finding a housekeeper. She was nursing Destiny one afternoon when she heard someone ring the doorbell. She knew that Cade was downstairs and would get it. She heard some commotion and thought it was someone delivering something that she had ordered. She heard footsteps coming up the stairs and reached for a blanket to cover her if necessary. When Cade came through the door, she asked, "Who was that at the door?" Cade smiled and answered, "It is someone that has made a long journey to see you." When Maria rounded the corner, Rebecca could not contain herself. She was overjoyed to see her. "Cade, how did you do this, baby!" She hugged Maria and watched as she admired Destiny. "I told you that all you had to do was but to request it, and if it were in my power, it would be granted." Maria smiled at both of them and said, "Thank you, senorita, for allowing me here. I will do my very best for you. I am filled with gladness for you and this little one," Maria said as she hugged her gently. Rebecca had a million questions and wanted to ask them all at once, but instead, she was thrilled that she was here. Cade went downstairs to show the limo driver where to put her things. Maria said, "The little princess is beautiful like her mother! Senor Cade is a very proud papa. He has a very good heart, and I am pleased that he found someone that suits him so well, Rebecca. You can feel the happiness when you walk through the doors. I am very pleased to see that you put all the ugliness behind you." Rebecca laid Destiny in her bassinet and pulled the doors so they could speak freely. "Maria, I am so thrilled that you are here with us. I wanted someone that I could depend on and trust. I feel very close to you, and I want you to know that you are more than an employee, you are part of our family. If there is anything you need or anything that will make you more comfortable, all you need to do is say so. I think that you and I should go downstairs and have a long talk. There are some things that you should know about me." Rebecca took Maria downstairs, and she began telling her all about how she was raised and of her family. Maria listened intently at all that Rebecca had told her. Maria had never heard of Amish people before, but in her country, there are people who live without any modern convenience at all because of being poor. She also explained to her how they dressed and what to expect. Maria reassured her that everything would be fine. She was just about through showing her where everything was when she remembered something. "Maria, there is one other thing, I have not told anyone other than Cade's mother about what happened in Mexico. I do not want anyone to know." Maria responded, "Of course, senorita." Cade came in at the end of the conversation and was pleased that Rebecca had already explained everything to her and had finished showing her around. "Maria, I will have carpenters here the Monday after Thanksgiving to start your apartment off the kitchen. I will draw the blueprints up myself, so if there is any special request that you might have, please let me know, and I will accommodate them." Maria had a few questions of her own. When they had planned everything out and decided on a menu, Rebecca explained that she and her family would be doing the majority of the meal. Maria was pleased with all the arrangements and was eager to call it a night.

Rebecca was amazed at how easy everything had gone together and very pleased at how fast Maria had caught on to her new surround. She sat in her room going through everything one more time when Cade came in the room. Cade laughed at her, watching Destiny sleep. Cade motioned for her to follow him. He held her hand, and together they walked downstairs. Rebecca saw a huge package standing against a wall in the foyer; she was puzzled at what it could be, when Cade unveiled it, Rebecca was lost for words. It was one of the pictures that the photographer had taken. Cade had had it framed and was about to have it hung over the staircase. He never stopped fulfilling her every wish. She wanted so badly for once to do something for him in return. She kissed him and said, "Cade, it is perfect! It is just as I pictured in my mind. Thank you so much for having this done for us. You are so very good to me." Cade instructed the men where it was supposed to be hung. Rebecca watched as the men did their job and was very pleased with the outcome. She could not take her eyes off the picture. She felt so blessed to have the perfect family.

CHAPTER 16

Rebecca thought her heart was going to jump out of her chest when she saw the van filled with her family coming up the drive. "Maria, they are here!" she yelled as she raced to the door. As everyone got out of the vehicle, she could not help but notice that everyone was smiling. Each one carried a basket of goodies and a cloth bag filled with extra cloths. Rebecca opened the door and welcomed them in. They were amazed at the size of the house and were even more amazed when they went inside. Rebecca wanted them to feel at home and was careful to make them feel as if they were. Maria had made a huge brunch, and the smell of fresh coffee permeated the whole house. Mary was in total loss for words when she reached the kitchen and saw all the modern appliances. She was so excited to be there and wanted the visit to go well for everyone. Rebecca showed them the house and told everyone where they would sleep. When everyone was settled in, they all returned to the kitchen for their first meal together. John and Kelly were delighted to find that Rebecca had bought two high chairs for the twins and were touched by her thoughtfulness. Rebecca introduced Maria and told them about how they first met. Cade watched as Rebecca was in heaven as she was surrounded by her whole family. He loved it too and laughed to himself at the thought of having to add on. By the time that all of Rebecca's brothers and sisters had children and the many more that he and Rebecca wanted, he might as well add another whole house on. Rebecca saw that he was smiling and, without saying a word, conveyed to him how much she loved him and how happy she was. They all ate and shared stories about things that had happened since they were all together. When the meal was over, everyone went into the living room to enjoy more conversation. Samuel, Cade, John, and David went on the back porch to look at the many pastures that were there, and the women discussed what they should cook first. The hours went by way too fast, and Rebecca could not believe that she was saying goodbye to her family so soon. She extended an invitation to do the same thing at Christmas, and everyone joyously accepted. She and Cade watched as the driver pulled down the driveway. The last few days had been long, and Rebecca was exhausted. She helped Maria pick up as much as she could before Cade told her to get some rest. Rebecca was too tired to argue and carried Destiny up and readied her for bed. Cade watched her hungrily as she removed her clothes and got in the shower. He pulled the covers down and crawled in bed. When Rebecca got out of the shower, she saw the hungry look he had and knew what his body ached for. She thought that it had been long enough, and her body had had adequate time to heal. She brushed her long wet hair and walked to the bed. Cade never took his eyes off her as she took her robe off and laid it at the foot of their bed. Rebecca crawled into bed and positioned herself so that she could kiss his black matted, hard chest. Cade sucked in his breath at the fire it was igniting. Cade captured her lips in a deep longing caress. Every inch of his body cried out for this woman, and she was inviting him. He quickly laid her under him, and he delivered feverish kisses to her pouty full lips. Rebecca's breathing became very fast, and at times, she held her breath at the feeling that was rising in her. He body moved in ways that begged him to take her. Cade's shaft was dancing with every beat of his heart. Rebecca could feel the hard, hot manhood as it teased her thigh. She wanted it inside her. Her body cried for the satisfaction that only Cade could give her. She wrapped her tiny hands around it and began to stroke it madly. Cade's body was taut with excitement. He wanted to plunge deep inside her and quench this thirst that only she could quench. It had been too long since he held her, and he begged his body for more precious time. He rubbed the mounds that were standing to attention and were filled with milk. He captured one of the hard peaks and began to suckle it. Rebecca cried in delight. Cade moved one hand to her dark hot, matted, secret place that was begging for his manhood. He could feel the flame of desire as it seared both of their bodies. Cade wanted to watch the flames of desire in her eyes as she was pleasured. He picked her up and, with one motion, had her sitting on top of him. He grabbed his long shaft and slid it gently inside of her. He was not prepared for the pleasure that it sent through him. Rebecca moaned loudly as his hard manhood thrust inside her. Cade loved watching her mounds dance at the force of his thrusts. It was when he saw a droplet of milk escape that he pulled her down to him and began to suckle from her breast. Cade drank thirstily from both of them as her milk came down and sprayed all over him. Cade's thrusts became harder and harder as he watched Rebecca's body quiver in delight. He watched as the flames of ecstasy overtook Rebecca's body, and it excited him fully. His body wrenched as his release came, and it jerked forcefully as his seed spilled deep inside her. When their bodies relaxed, she lay quietly on his chest. Cade held her close to him and so glad that he could finally hold her intimately. It amazed him that he had gone for years without a woman, but he could not make it four weeks without Rebecca. His body craved for her. She was just as necessary as the air he breathed. He thought of the passionate love they had just made and was not surprised as his body ached for her again. He took her again and made love to her slowly, enjoying every inch of her magnificent body. When the morning sun was peaking through the horizon, they finally lay sated in each other's arms. The intensity of their lovemaking always shook his soul. The more they visited that intimate place, the more it became necessary. Their love had been taken to new levels, and it was never-ending. Even as he lay there with her in his arms after making love all night, he could honestly say that he had not had his fill of her. He listened to her breathing, and it sang him to sleep. They were awakened to the sound of Destiny crying, and Cade got up to get her. He changed her diaper and handed her to Rebecca to feed. He watched as Destiny nursed hungrily at her mother's breast. He relived the memories of last night and the way that he had done the same thing. He rubbed Rebecca's face and said, "I know you are tired, baby, when you are finished, I will lay her down, and you can just stay in bed if you want. I will tell Maria that you are going to sleep for a while." Rebecca smiled sleepily and said, "Destiny can sleep in my arms, and yes, I would love to sleep for a while." Cade went downstairs and told Maria not to prepare breakfast; when he came back upstairs and saw Rebecca asleep with Destiny at her breast, his eyes filled with tears at the beauty of it. He sat next to them and marveled at the precious sight. He gently snuggled next to them and quickly fell back asleep.

The sun had reached midday, and Rebecca awoke to a wonderful smell that could only mean that Maria was cooking lunch. Her stomach rumbled in protest to her sleeping in. Rebecca nursed Destiny and carried her downstairs; Cade was not in the bed and thought he would be in the kitchen as well. Rebecca followed the wonderful smell to the kitchen and laid Destiny in a bassinet that had been placed there. "Good morning, Maria. What is that wonderful smell? I am starving," she stated. Maria looked at her with a mischievous smile and said, "Sit and I will prepare your plate, senorita. I hope that you rested well last night." Rebecca knew exactly what she meant. "Senor Cade left a little bit ago, and might I say, he was very jovial this morning." Rebecca smiled innocently at Maria's remark. "We may have another bambino very soon, senorita," Maria said jokingly. Rebecca looked at her and made a face. "Would that be so bad?" Maria said, "Not at all, senorita, I was just teasing you. However, it is easier for you to get pregnant after a girl baby than it is after a boy baby. That is one of those secrets that a doctor will not tell you, but it is so." Rebecca laughed and did not take her seriously at all. She thought that Maria was teasing her. "Where did Cade say he was going, Maria?" "He was on the phone with the contractor that is to build the apartment for me. He went to bring the plans for him to look at. He said to tell you that he loves you more and more each day and that he would not be long." Rebecca ate her lunch thinking about what Cade was doing. He had not mentioned anything to her about having to go somewhere. When she had finished, she returned upstairs with Destiny to get them both dressed for the day. She played and cuddled with Destiny and lost all track of time. When she heard the front door slam, she realized that it was midafternoon. She heard Maria tell him that she was upstairs. Cade opened the door and saw her and Destiny lying across the bed. "Hello, my darling," he said as he rushed to lay by her side. "Did you get some rest?" "Yes, I did. In fact, we slept till noon," she said, smiling. Cade nuzzled her ear and whispered, "You deserved it. You worked very hard last night." She giggled at the implication and watched as Cade gave a tender kiss to their daughter. "I knew you would probably sleep for a while and took the opportunity to get those plans for the apartment to Dave Jemison, the contractor. We are also discussing an addition to the whole back of the house. When I saw how full the house was at Thanksgiving, I realized that when David, Amos, and Paul have kids and Steven, Sarah, Katie, and Annie have kids and all that we are going to have, we will be packed like sardines in a can in here. I will draw some plans up and show you what I have in mind." It thrilled Rebecca immensely to know Cade was planning on having more meals together and wanted to make it as comfortable as it could be. "Mother said that David is going to announce his intentions next week. Although I may not attend the wedding, I would like to get them a gift. He is going to marry Daniel's youngest sister," she explained. "Will that make you uncomfortable, Bec?" he asked worriedly. "No, not at all. She is very sweet, but we never had a friendship. I am very excited for him, and you are right, when all my brothers and sisters have families of their own, we will really have the house full." Cade kissed her lips softly and said in a husky voice, "Many nights like last night and we will have another member to *our* family soon!" Rebecca kissed him passionately and replied, "Who says we have to wait till nighttime?" Cade kissed her and allowed his tongue to search her pouting, parted lips. He looked into her eyes as he tasted her sweetness and replied, "No one at all." He untied her robe and lifted her from the bed. He gently picked up his sleeping daughter and laid her in her bed. He hurriedly removed his clothes, and when he returned to her, he pressed his body next to her until she was captured by the bed. He slowed her fall and rubbed the length of her bare back. When she lay beneath him, he became breathless with her beauty. He admired her body hungrily as she guided his swollen member deep into her womb. Cade teased her by giving her only short, little millimeters of his shaft. Rebecca moved her hips to try to gain the whole length. When she saw that her efforts were in vain, she captured his bottom lip and sucked it as she wrapped her hands around his tight buttocks and pulled him forcefully deeper inside her. The pleasure was breathtaking, and Cade said breathlessly, "What do you want, Rebecca?" Rebecca looked him in the eye, and while licking his lips, she stared at him lustfully and answered, "I want you to give me another baby." The implication that he was breeding her drove him wild. He took her passionately. So passionately that he was sure that Maria had heard them. He plunged deeper and deeper inside her until they both exploded into a kaleidoscope of ecstasy. They lay breathless as they traveled back to reality. Cade caressed her gently as they were watching their most priceless gift.

 The next few weeks were filled with love and family. They were planning a huge Christmas, and they both felt privileged to have such a wonderful life. Destiny continued to grow, and she gave the most beautiful smiles that either had ever seen. Rebecca wanted to give Cade something very special for Christmas. She could not think of anything that he would want, and it was bothering her. It was not until she had gotten up queasy one morning that the possibility of an impending pregnancy hit her. She had informed Maria and requested that she add a pregnancy test to her list of things to purchase this week. She asked her not to say anything until she knew for sure. When the grocer made its delivery, Maria got it out and took it upstairs. Rebecca waited till Cade was occupied in his study and took the test. When it came up positive, immediately she was thrilled. She wanted to tell him in a very special way; the excitement was hard to keep to herself. When Christmas morning finally arrived, Cade gathered everyone around the huge, twenty-foot-tall Christmas tree that they had all decorated the evening before. Cade passed out gifts, and when everyone was busy opening what had been handed to them, Cade handed a small box to Rebecca. When she opened it and pulled the contents out of the small box, it was an incredibly beautiful bracelet. It had diamonds that alternated with charms that were to be filled with the birthstones of their children. He had placed a nice size Mexican opal on the first birthstone slot in commemoration of Destiny's birth. Cade slipped it on Rebecca's wrist and asked, "Do you like it, my darling?" Rebecca admired the bracelet as it lay on her wrist. She loved the delicate craftsmanship that obviously took the crafter some time to make. However, she loved what it represented more than anything. She would wear this to show her commitment to Cade and her children. She kissed Cade's lips with the utmost tenderness and answered, "It is exquisite, Cade. I will wear it with pride because it shows where my heart belongs." Rebecca added softly, "I must tell you that you will need to take it back to the jeweler soon however, my love." Rebecca watched as the realization hit him. "Oh my god, baby! You are pregnant?" he asked excitedly. Rebecca smiled and nodded her head. Cade held her close to him and kissed her sweet lips. "I love you," he said breathlessly. He stood and announced to their family that by next Christmas, there would be another little one joining them.